MR. WOLF
V.
THE THREE PIGS

MARIE GUILLAUME *&* WILLIAM GUILLAUME

This book or any portion thereof
may not be reproduced or used in any manner whatsoever
without the express written permission of the publisher or authors
except for the use of brief quotations in a book review.

Copyright © 2013 Marie and William Guillaume
All Rights Reserved.

ISBN-10: 0615706339
ISBN-13: 9780615706337

"A book is proof that humans are capable of working magic."

– Carl Sagan

ACKNOWLEDGEMENTS

We would like to dedicate this book to all the parents and educators who continue to fan the flame of creativity in children.

We would like to thank our children Fedon, Achieng, and AJ who allowed us to finish this book. We love you.

We are grateful to our creative editing and legal team for believing in **Mr. Wolf v. The Three Pigs**. *Thank you for assisting us in making it a reality- Cherilyn Williams, Regine Pointdujour, Yadhira Gonzalez-Taylor, Lorna Jerome, Erika Harvey, Maryana Lukanjuk, and Fern Dejong.*

We would like to thank Erika Harvey so much for her support. Words cannot express our thanks.

We would like to thank Vincent Gravelli for all his support.

We owe a big debt to our earliest readers: Erika Bantecourt, Mylikqua Corbett, Jahro, Christian, and Kurtis Minter who gave us the motivation to continue Mr. Wolf v.The Three Pigs.

We would like to thank our young reader and special assistant, Aaliyah Rosa Taylor, for helping us to see the characters through the eyes of our future readers.

Thank you, Heavenly Cruz for bringing Mr. Wolf to life.

Thanks You, Ms. Ursula Chase for your advice and support.

To all our Facebook fans who pressed the Like Button on **Mr. Wolf v The Three Pigs** Fan page and provide support as we continue to build Mr. Wolf's fan base. We thank you for your support. Here are some of Mr. Wolf's most supportive fans:

Tricia Latham Trainer, Dren Telaku, Melinda Cochrane, Bongkot Chayayen, Erlene King, Dawn Kruger–Gode, Minnie Seferaj, Justin Miller, Josh Kevin James, Megyn James, Nathan McCain, Emmie McGuire, Lyla Miller, Vanina Lopez James, Ryan Mitchell, Alicia Fernandez-Mitchell, Hannah Norrish Bush, Tommy Parker, Melanie Myers, Anise Dixon, Delia Rojas, Sierra Price, Michelle Diaz, Melkie McCalla, Beatriz Tinoco, Korab Agolli, Provide Support LLC, Carolyn Bland, Lucas Okinyi, Wady El-Nino, Avi Persidi, Roan Wynter, Jerome Hall, Trina Maynard, Noely Cruz, Glorie Boodoo, Ernest Morgan, Zagada Cyrus, Robert Sotillio, Patrick Rhoden, Alonzo Golden, Chris Anderson, Keith Brown, John Cerjak, Robert Turner, Vincent Oliver, Brian Jack, Chris Anderson, Eco Global Society, Wilson Astudillo, Donald Wenz, Kia Washington, Chermain Miller, Nicola Jane Cleverley, Sonya Raymond, Tiffany Murray, Lisa Fran, Mandy J Corry, Emmanuel Frank, Monica Johnson, Shawn McDonald, Lizzie Sharman, Ali Lickert, Mellisa Persaud, Tyrone Steward, Eslon Bennett, Natasha Applewhite, Ismael Aguirre, Joe Cooper, Alicia Capano, Althea Beckford, Helen Morgan, Maggie Martin, Chris Arizmendi, Kikie Edogawa, Cherrie Johnson, Tiffany Weynard, Trevor Harris, Devon Whitter, Tafari Sherry, Ed David, Luiz Marrieno, Nicola Roach, Naomi Paige, Junior Rebollo, Curtis Brown, Rashawn Harris, Daniela Messi, Nigel John Kirkman, Eslon Bennet, Samanta Tiwari, Billy Ctid Marshall, Val Valeria, and Zukas Jung.

We would also like to thank the rest of our **Facebook fans** who are too many to name.

Thank You, from Mr. Wolf and Associates:

To our parents who gave us life

To my colleagues in the Criminal Justice, Business, Medical, Computer, General Arts and Science Department who work tirelessly not because of the money, but because of our passion for teaching.

To our family and friends who supported us in this endeavor

To Melkie McCalla and Thamar Mendez.

To the lawyers who fight for justice every day.

To those in law enforcement for their service.

To those with a creative spirit: we say; "free your mind and just write."

To John Jay College of Criminal Justice.

To all the veterans and active service men and women.

To Brooklyn College for all your support.

To my law school for preparing me to think.

To my law school classmates and Facebook friends who allowed me to tag their pages.

To all my soccer friends around the world.

To all my students who made my life a much richer and fulfilling adventure.

This book is dedicated to the memory of my dog, Flash, and to all animal lovers everywhere.

Finally, we dedicate this book in memory of those who left us: Lazarus Guillaume, Levy Washington, Terry-Ann Llewellyn–Corniffe, Alex Claes, and Eli Joseph.

Please like us on Facebook @ Mr. Wolf v The Three Pigs if you wish to follow discussions and events for Mr. Wolf.

INTRODUCTION

A s the sun rose on a clear crisp, fall morning, Mr. Wolf glanced at the grandfather clock across the room. The clock reminded Mr. Wolf that time was in fact running out for him. As the hands moved precisely and mechanically, Mr. Wolf lay alone on his old bamboo twin-sized bed and quietly reflected on the life and the legacy he would leave behind for his heirs. The years had not been kind to Mr. Wolf, since now he needed a cane when his hind leg acted up. His leg often pained him, especially when rain was in the air. What was left of his once-thick brown hair was now mostly white, especially around the temples. He always carried a white handkerchief to mop the sweat that profusely beaded his bald pate mostly in the hot summer months.

Glaucoma blurred his vision, so the square-rimmed glasses perched on his face helped him see things clearer. He had gained considerable weight around his midsection, so he sported the most colorful suspenders to keep his pants securely at his waist. Some would call it a paunch, but Mr. Wolf's rounded stomach was the least of his troubles. Mr. Wolf was getting older, and some issues from his past were casting a dark cloud on his future and the future of the other wolves in the pack. While some might argue that what happened in the past should stay in the past, Mr. Wolf knew he would never get a moment of peace until he resolved this particular issue. This particular problem had tormented him for a long time, and it was finally time to do something about it.

Mr. Wolf was much older and wiser than he was all those years ago when he had that fateful encounter with the pigs, but the incident with The Three Little Pigs still haunted him. Not only had the pigs lied on him, but their lies also had reverberated throughout the whole wolf community, the pig community, the animal kingdom, and most troubling, all over the world. It was the main reason Mr. Wolf stayed up many nights, and why he was up so early this morning contemplating his next move. Mr. Wolf knew everyone believed The Three Pigs' lies, but Mr. Wolf knew better. He had to clear his name. It was a long shot, but clearing his name had become his obsession. *What wolf with integrity would not defend his honor*, thought Mr. Wolf as he shuffled around restlessly in bed, trying to gather his thoughts. He was tired of everyone following him and stigmatizing him as that *big bad wolf*. However, it would take some time before he was ready to act.

CHAPTER ONE

STICKS AND STONES MAY BREAK MY BONES, BUT WORDS CAN ALSO HURT

Several weeks later, on a rather dismal and rainy morning, Mr. Wolf awoke to a slight tingle in his leg and torrents of rain battering the solitary window by the right side of his bed. Minutes later, he climbed out of his warm cocoon and began pacing back and forth in his old one-room rectangular-shaped house that was badly in need of repair. The wood-burning stove quickly pushed out the damp air creeping steadily beneath the door. The old rickety log cabin stood on a high ridge in the heart of the woods, tucked away from pedestrian traffic at the end of a dead-end road. The house, neglected by the passage of time, had lost some of its color over the years. Mr. Wolf's house remained hidden from the occasional sunlight by the tall trees and vines that enveloped it, thus preventing the windows from capturing the natural light. The roof of the house was covered in turf grass that preserved the cool intimacy and coziness that Mr. Wolf treasured, especially during the spring and summer months. The now-muddied path leading up to the dark-green painted rectangular door with its oval brass knocker was covered on both sides by towering trees with leaves that waved violently in the powerful winds.

The inside of the small house had become old with the passage of time and quartered off into sections by dark green curtains set on a pulley system. The thick threadbare curtains made the house appear shabbier and smaller than it was. As Mr. Wolf paced around the small sparsely furnished bedroom, which held two twin-sized bamboo beds and a bamboo dresser neatly stacked with socks and undergarments, he walked over toward the dresser and absentmindedly fiddled with the cosmetics that sat atop its smooth surface. He became more agitated as his heavy paws made loud squeaky sounds on the uneven wooden floor, waking Mrs. Wolf from her early-morning slumber. Her red-checkered sleeping cap sat on her head, tied with a bow under her chin. Mrs. Wolf's salt-and-pepper hair, pulled back in an awkward ponytail, rested on her shoulders. She popped her head up from her feathered pillow and pulled her blanket tighter around her slender form. She peered at the antique clock directly across from her bed through half-closed eyes and saw it was still quite early. What could it be now? Mrs. Wolf wondered sleepily as she yawned loudly. As the pacing continued, the squeaking became louder and louder, and Mrs. Wolf could no longer ignore it. She was becoming increasingly irritated because she had planned to sleep a little later on such a cold and dreary day, but with the racket Mr. Wolf was making, sleep was impossible. "What is the problem now?" Mrs. Wolf asked, almost afraid to hear the answer as she rolled out of bed. Her grey flannel nightgown kept some of the morning chill at bay as she sauntered lazily over to the yellow basin at the foot of her bed. She brushed her sensitive teeth gingerly, and a slight grimace briefly skirted across her face as she scrubbed away the bitter taste of morning breath that lingered in her mouth.

"You know what the problem is, I have to clear my name," Mr. Wolf replied in a heavy, raspy voice that had once been a distinctive commanding bass voice, but had changed with the passage of time. He turned around, stared at the back of Mrs. Wolf's head, and braced himself for the usual confrontation that occurred each time he brought the subject up.

"Well, if you ask me, I think you should just forget it," said Mrs. Wolf, who had finished brushing her teeth, knowing exactly what he was thinking.

"Well, I didn't ask you," said Mr. Wolf quite gruffly as he stared Mrs. Wolf down. The tension in the old drafty room had become quite uneasy, as this issue with the pigs had been a cause of disagreement between them over the years.

"Mr. Wolf, I think it would be best for all concerned if you let this foolish idea go," said Mrs. Wolf in a condescending tone. This made Mr. Wolf angry. Mrs. Wolf always brushed him off when it came to this matter, but this time he was not about to let that happen.

"NO! NO! I WILL NOT FORGET IT!" yelled Mr. Wolf as he stamped his feet like a petulant child upset about not getting his way. "I am going to clear my name because the older I get, the more it is bothering me. You just don't understand how tired I am of everyone thinking I am the '*big bad wolf.*'" Can't you see that these three little pigs' lies have destroyed the reputation of all wolves? Don't you care?" Mr. Wolf asked, trying to get Mrs. Wolf to see his point of view. Mr. Wolf was angry.

Mrs. Wolf glared back at her husband, tired of his foolishness. In exasperation, she threw her front paws in the air and said, "Why are you still calling them little pigs? Have you seen them lately? They are not the little pigs you remember. You are still stuck in the past, Mr. Wolf, so it is useless arguing with you anyway." Mrs. Wolf sighed, and took a deep breath before she totally lost her temper. She had put the past behind her, and she wished Mr. Wolf would listen to her and do the same. Furthermore, who cared what three smelly pigs said anyway? Mrs. Wolf thought as she again took a deep breath and counted to three, trying to maintain her cool. Some of Mr. Wolf's anger dissipated as he tried to persuade her about the importance of clearing his name. He patted her ever so slightly on the shoulder, gazing intently into her eyes, but Mrs. Wolf pushed his paw away impatiently and screamed, "OH, GET OVER IT, WOLFIE! Please leave the children and me out of it. We couldn't care less about some old idiotic pig story." When it appeared Mrs. Wolf was not budging from her position, Mr. Wolf grew silent.

Finally he said, "I am going to clear my name and the name of the generation of wolves to come, whether you are with me or not."

"Well, how are you going to do that, my dear Wolfie?" Mrs. Wolf asked, looking quite puzzled. This was the most determined she had seen Mr. Wolf, and she wondered if he really was serious about clearing his name.

"Well, early Monday morning, I will be going down to the Law Office of Honest Pig and Honest Pig," said Mr. Wolf. Before he could finish speaking, Mrs. Wolf burst out laughing, "Oh, ha, ha, ha, ha."

"STOP IT, STOP IT, YOU STOP LAUGHING AT ME!" shouted Mr. Wolf.

"Oh, Sorry! Sorry!" Mrs. Wolf said sarcastically. "I am sorry for thinking you're silly, but that is the craziest idea I have ever heard. Do you really think those darn pigs are going to represent you?" Mrs. Wolf held her chest as if she were in pain.

"Well, if they're honest, they will represent us," Mr. Wolf replied heatedly as he glared at Mrs. Wolf to emphasize the seriousness of his intentions.

"*Us! Us!* What do you mean *Us*?" Mrs. Wolf asked, moving aggressively toward Mr. Wolf as if she was about to attack him for suggesting she would be involved in this debacle. "I am proud to be a wolf. If they want to think I am a '*big bad wolf*' let them think that. I really do not care one way or the other." Mrs. Wolf stopped abruptly in front of Mr. Wolf while stamping her feet.

"Gosh, Wolfie, you just get under my fur with this nonsense. Furthermore, pigs are pigs and wolves are wolves. We are different, and we will always be different, Nature intended for us to be different, and so it is, so who cares what these pigs think of us?" Mrs. Wolf began to plead with Mr. Wolf. "Wolfie, please! You must forget this whole thing. Nobody cares anymore, forget it." When she realized she was not getting through to Mr. Wolf, she said with an air of finality and defiance, "I am not going to any pig to get help; that is just not the way this wolf rolls."

CHAPTER ONE

In righteous indignation, Mr. Wolf glared at Mrs. Wolf and raised up on his hind paws, assuming an air of authority his wife had never witnessed before, and bellowed, "Well, I'm the head of the pack, and I am going to stand up to these lying pigs if it's the last thing I do!" He pounded the floor repeatedly with his left hind paw in an obvious sign of frustration. "Furthermore, HP and HP is my secret weapon. Think about it, Mrs. Wolf, what better way to expose those lying pigs than through a high-powered pig attorney, one of their own kind!" By then, he had worked himself into a frenzy, huffing and puffing breathlessly as he talked.

Mrs. Wolf glared at Mr. Wolf one last time before she turned around and stormed out of the bedroom, disgusted with his stubborn decision to carry the whole wolf pack into this old character battle. As she left the room, Mrs. Wolf thought that Mr. Wolf sure had the nerve to huff and puff, because it was huffing and puffing that had put him in this predicament in the first place. Mrs. Wolf wondered uneasily if her husband was serious about this confrontation with the pigs. She wondered if he had a strategy for winning this case. Especially considering that, public opinion was overwhelmingly in favor of the pigs. These unsettling thoughts haunted Mrs. Wolf throughout the coming days.

CHAPTER TWO

COUNSEL OF WOLVES

Mr. Wolf scheduled a meeting with the Counsel of Wolves (COW), which often debated matters of importance in the wolf community. As he trudged through the dimly lit forest to make this appointment, packs of wolves crunched together under an umbrella of trees in the dark and nearly deserted forest. Only the brave of heart dared to venture into this isolated and feared habitat, but today the wolves found safety in numbers. The temperature had dipped unusually low, so many of them bundled under their coats as they waited listlessly for Mr. Wolf. The younger wolves on the outskirts of the pack waited impatiently as they struggled to get reception on their cell phones to summon missing wolves in case they needed solidarity against some stupid plan the older folks were about to enforce. The older wolves huddled closer as they greeted one another with wolf pounds while contemplating the reason for the meeting. A few feet away, another group of wolves formed a seamless circle and engaged in mindless chatter as they awaited the preliminaries to get underway. Everyone knew something serious was about to transpire, but Mr. Wolf had been quite evasive when he sent word concerning the meeting. They just had to wait on him to appease their curiosity.

Many of the wolves had gotten wind of the council via the customary triple howl that echoed through the woods signifying an emergency meeting. The older wolves had started the tradition and continued with it despite the prevalence of new technology. The younger wolves preferred phones, but the ear-shattering howls were difficult to ignore. At lightning speed, the word had ricocheted through the woods and its outskirts, where many of the wolves resided cut off from the hustle and bustle of the economic engine of the city.

Before the meeting commenced, a loud "Ahwoo, ahwoo" signaling Mr. Wolf's approach alerted the company of his arrival. Packs of wolves cleared a path as other youthful wolves, who feared being late, sped up on their mopeds. Each rider had a single toothpick protruding from his mouth, scattering pebbles and fallen leaves in their wake. Older wolves upset at the cavalier attitude of the younger wolves spoke in hushed and halting tones decrying the disrespect of the younger generation.

Silence blanketed the meeting area as Mr. Wolf made his way through the crowd, greeting fellow wolves as he walked to the front of the gathering. Streaks of flickering orange sunlight filtered through the evening shadows that had settled on the dense woods, thus creating a somber mood. As Mr. Wolf proceeded to take his place, he seemed to assume an air of authority and strength of purpose never before witnessed by the wolf community. This new posture was different from the defeated look and slouched gait that had become him in the past. One solitary ray of sunlight beamed a spotlight around him as he stood majestically at center stage.

"This is a sure sign of something momentous, and I am already proud to be part of whatever it is," muttered one wolf. The merging of the tall trees created the perfect canopy to house the meeting amidst the litter of the yellow brown leaves and twigs that formed a quilt-like carpet flooring for the damp earth.

There was some chattering and shuffling when Mr. Wolf assumed his position. He took a few moments to adjust his glasses and then he surveyed the audience keenly before raising his front paws to get their attention. He pondered his next move thoughtfully for a few moments, and then said:

Fellow council members, and brothers of the wolf community, I have convened this meeting today to declare war on our tormentors. It has been far too long that we, the wolves, have been labeled as dangerous predators. We have been under attack and hunted like wild animals by the citizens and State of Maplewood. For decades, this community has endured the scorn of society, and it is time to take back our pride, our reputation, our good name, and our legacy, which the pigs stole from us. After The Three Pigs falsely accused me, I suffered, you suffered, and our children have suffered. As president, I can no longer sit back and accept the disenfranchisement of our children. We are victims of a decadent society devoid of fair conscience or goodwill toward us. For years, I felt helpless to fight back, but today I stand before you as your president ready to pursue the justice that has long eluded us. I am taking my case to court, and I am here to seek your support. The time is right, and our cause is just. Let us right this terrible wrong for the sake of our posterity and for the future of the wolf community.

When Mr. Wolf finished speaking, the wolves fell silent. A few nodded their heads in partial agreement, but most of them watched him incredulously. By then dusk had settled over the woods, crickets began chirping, and birds had settled in their nests. The darkness of the woods made the packs of wolves almost invisible, and the only evidence of their presence was their sharply piercing eyes that seemed to light up the night like fireflies. In the foreboding darkness of the eerie woods, a few white furs commingled with the dominant dark and brown furs that seemed to fuse together as testament to the might of wolf power. They would stand together for their rights but not quite the way Mr. Wolf expected. He sensed an underlying obstinacy that was not about to yield to his wishes.

Mr. Wolf had come to the counsel to discuss his decision to clear his name. However, now he was not sure that had been a good idea as many of the wolves broke their silence and began to howl at the thought of him clearing his name. One younger wolf in particular, who was young and agile the way Mr. Wolf had been when he was younger, sneered at the thought of Mr. Wolf clearing his name. The younger wolf, nicknamed Stalker because of his hunting abilities, asked Mr. Wolf, "Why would you do that?" in a contemptuous tone. "Why should we wolves care what some dumb pigs think? Our reputation is fine the way it is, President Wolf!" continued Stalker, walking to the front as he eye-balled Mr. Wolf while proudly patting the mop of black fur on his head shaped into a stylish buzz cut. Stalker considered himself quite the ladies wolf, and today he was dressed to impress. He looked quite sinister in his black leather pants complemented by a black leather jacket with the word *Stalker* emblazoned on the back.

"Matter of fact, I kind of like being thought of as the '*big bad wolf.*'" He pounded his broad chest with his right paw and sized Mr. Wolf up disdainfully. "It seems to me, President Wolf, that you have lost your touch," mocked Stalker, daring to say what some of the other wolves were thinking but afraid to say. Most in the wolf community respected Mr. Wolf and held him in high esteem. "How many of our fellow citizens in the animal kingdom can say that the path is cleared when they walk down the street, stand in line at the bank, or merely stroll through the park? I call this ultimate respect, and I rather like it." At this statement, many of the younger council members responded with howls, whistles, back slaps, and high fives as they paw-slapped each other in agreement with Stalker.

Some of the other wolves were annoyed at Mr. Wolf, and thought he should have eaten The Three Pigs. At least no witnesses would have been left behind, and Mr. Wolf would not have to go to court to clear his name. One wolf at the back of the pack with a black patch over his right eye spoke up in a high soprano pitch voicing the very sentiment every-one believed, but did not dare articulate.

"Mr. Wolf, you should have just eaten the—" but he was drowned out by the loud howls and laughter from other wolves.

"What is this I hear about you having a pig representing you?" chimed in another wolf who was also peeved at Mr. Wolf.

CHAPTER TWO

"SAY IT ISN'T SO, MR. WOLF!" shouted a sly fox sitting in the front row.

Mr. Wolf had no response as the other wolves stared at him quite bewildered. He felt cornered as the wolves all tried to voice their opinions at once, making it extremely difficult to hear what they were saying. Maybe talking to the wolf pack had not been such a good idea, thought Mr. Wolf, hoping that this meeting would be over soon. Throughout the meeting, many of the wolves continued to voice their displeasure at what Mr. Wolf was about to do. Many hours later, he left the meeting feeling alone, dejected, and isolated from his peers. However, he knew what he had to do. Despite popular opinion, he needed to clear his name for the sake of his legacy, and no one would deter him from the task. To cheer himself up he muttered to himself, "Uneasy lays the head that wears the crown." He was going to see that Pig lawyer despite what everyone said. Mr. Wolf glanced at his old black watch, hoping it was not too late to call and set up an appointment.

CHAPTER THREE

TIME TO MEET THE LAWYER

Early on Monday morning, days after his meeting with the Council of Wolves, Mr. Wolf scrambled out of his warm bed. He was cautious not to disturb Mrs. Wolf, who was in a deep sleep, her snores vibrating throughout the small bedroom. Mr. Wolf looked at the clock and saw it was still quite early. He donned a light-blue shirt with striped slacks and teamed it with his colorful suspenders. Today his outfit was quite a contrast to his customary black and grey-colored wardrobe, and already he felt like a different wolf with a new purpose. He hastily scribbled a note explaining his destination and taped the note to the mirror, knowing that Mrs. Wolf spent many minutes gazing into it as if it held the secrets to eternal life. He silently exited the room, shut the front door behind him, and locked it with a single key before setting off for the City of Maplewood.

Mr. Wolf was loudly whistling a merry tune to buoy his spirits as he headed through the woods, encountering a few wolves on their way to work and school as he headed to the city. Mr. Wolf was used to walking. Many knew him for his ability to walk miles and miles through the dense forest. While he usually admired the beautiful green scenery, today he hardly noticed the changing of the colorful foliage, nor did he feel the crisp wisp of the fresh autumn air, or see the furry creatures that darted in and out of the bush as he contemplated what lay ahead. As he rounded a corner, he paused for a while to catch his breath under a huge chestnut tree, when an acorn fell on his head and startled him. Mr. Wolf looked up to see a squirrel scurrying away with a mischievous grin on his face. Mr. Wolf shook a warning paw at him and resumed his journey.

The footpath sloped suddenly down a hill that bordered the wishing pond where most of the wolves came to draw water in the dry season. Old Mr. Toad, resting comfortably on a large shamrock leaf, croaked loudly, "Beware the ides of November! Beware the demons that walk abroad." Mr. Toad was famous for his dire warnings as the seer in Maplewood, and he made Mr. Wolf most uncomfortable. Mr. Wolf tried to ignore him and picked up his pace, which turned into a brisk jog until he was out of earshot of Mr. Toad's unwanted rant. Mr. Wolf wondered whether this evil omen spelled defeat for him and his cause.

As he walked a little farther, Mr. Wolf felt as if the weight of a generation of wolves rested on his shoulders. Nevertheless, it seemed the closer he got to the city, the lighter his heart felt. When he neared the bustling City of Maplewood filled with pedestrians moving at various speeds, he put a smile on his face, something he had not done in years since the pigs' accusations had spread like wildfire. He watched in fascination as the urbanites sped by in their mini vans, jeeps, and two-door cars. Environmentally conscious pigs, rabbits, and wolves pedaled on their green two-wheeled cycles with helmets on their heads while others hurried to their final destination on foot. Mr. Wolf knew smiling would make him appear less scary, so he smiled and nodded to everyone he met along the way, whispering softly to himself, "I am going to clear my name. I am going to clear my name."

Most of the pedestrians on the streets were pigs, and many whispered among themselves and eyed Mr. Wolf suspiciously. One pig who looked past her prime whispered loudly to another pig as she pointed to Mr. Wolf, "Look at this wolf in sheep's clothing. I wonder who he is trying to fool now." Some of the pedestrians who heard this comment snickered as Mr. Wolf headed their way. The rumors and the cruel gossip had kept Mr. Wolf away from town.

Yet now, Mr. Wolf felt forced to relive the painful memories of yesteryears. In some of the store windows owned by pigs, Mr. Wolf's picture, bearing a striking resemblance to a criminal mug shot, still hung as a grim reminder to many in the pig community of the story of _The Three Little Pigs_. Mr. Wolf tried to appear as harmless as possible by smiling and waving, especially to the pigs that crossed his path, but unfortunately he was ostracized within the pig community and nothing was about to change that.

Many of the pigs ignored him, some sped up, and others clutched their belongings as they eyed Mr. Wolf defiantly. Some of the younger piglets on their way to school were dressed in their school uniforms. Mr. Wolf was pleasantly surprised because their well-pressed white ruffled blouses appeared tucked neatly into their navy-blue pleated skirts, and their socks very white. They even wore black shiny patent-leather shoes. Mr. Wolf stared in shock and disbelief at the blue and white ribbons neatly intertwined in their many pigtails.

The piglets began to shriek in horror as Mr. Wolf crossed their paths. Their parents had inundated them with stories of the "_big bad wolf_," and they were terrified at the way he was looking at them. Pandemonium broke lose as the piglets ran screaming down the street, scattering their books and lunch pails.

"Please, little piglets do not be afraid," one adult pig, admonished.

"Look at the '_big bad wolf_' now; he is just a shadow of his former self," the heavyset pig dressed in a nursing uniform said as she pointed at Mr. Wolf's cane while many of the older pigs laughed mockingly. Noting the pigs' reactions, Mr. Wolf remembered why he had to clear his name, and he hated being the center of attention. The wolves he encountered either exchanged fist pounds with him or nodded their heads in acknowledgment as he passed them.

Like a wolf on a mission, he picked up his gait, and walked the last blocks to the lawyer's office purposefully. He knew it was time to set the record straight, for he could feel the urgency in his bones. He was definitely getting too old, and his heart was too weak to carry this heavy burden. He also knew he had to relieve the nagging pain of emotional distress that had haunted him over the years before putting the matter to rest.

When Mr. Wolf reached the antique African mahogany cherry-stained round-top double door with raised moldings of the Law Office of Honest Pig and Honest Pig, he began to feel extremely nervous. He stared at the red and white billboard hoisted near the roof that denoted the services of the law office. He quickly took note of the motto on the sign, "**Every client is our priority.**" Mr. Wolf felt a little better as he read the sign, but still he paced up and down the three steps in front of the law office before he summoned the courage to knock on the door. Again, he wondered if it was wise to come to a pig for help.

As he stood outside the door, he remembered Mrs. Wolf's earlier query, "Why don't you forget about this whole thing?" He also saw the wolves' angry faces from the council and heard their voices as they asked, "Why are you going to those pigs for help?" Mr. Wolf also remembered the terror on the faces of the young piglets as they huddled in horror, while other pigs laughed and whispered as he passed them on the way to the law office. Instantly, he also remembered the lies that The Three Pigs had told on him, so he pummeled the door loudly with his cane. Bang! Bang! However, no one answered him. He sat on the steps of the law office feeling very dejected and disheartened. He had an appointment, so where was this pig attorney, he wondered. He wondered if the attorney had changed his mind about representing him. Despite these troubling thoughts, Mr. Wolf decided to knock one last time. He got up and knocked three times louder than before and shouted, "Honest Pigs, Honest Pigs, may I come in?"

Finally, a stately looking black boar twice his height opened the door, looking quite perturbed. "Why didn't you ring the bell?" the Boar asked, pointing to the ringer located to the right of the door, as he stared at Mr. Wolf curiously. His smooth melodious voice was quite a contrast to his looming figure. Then without waiting for an answer, the imposing black boar politely said, "Come on in," and introduced himself as the receptionist for the Law Office of Honest Pig and Honest Pig.

"I have an appointment with Counsel Boar, and I am Mr. Wolf," he said.

"I know; we were expecting you," replied the black boar.

The boar had a neatly trimmed black mustache, but he was dressed more like a butler than a receptionist. The black boar pressed the intercom on the wall and said, "Mr. Wolf is here, sir."

A muffled grunt echoed gruffly through the system, "Very good, let him come in." The black boar led the way through a brightly lit hallway, and Mr. Wolf looked admiringly at the lime green walls along the corridor that complemented a red accent panel.

They proceeded to the reception area, and as they passed through the open door, the sight that met Mr. Wolf's eye shattered his perception of what a lawyer's office should look like. He expected order; instead, Mr. Wolf saw what some would call chaos. While Mr. Wolf did not say it aloud, he felt the office looked a little too piggish. There seemed to be more books than walls. The office had papers piled on the floor, on top of the desk, and on top of the file cabinets. Empty juice boxes and stale leftover food sat carelessly strewn on a tiny eating table in the corner of the hallway. This was what one would expect from pigs anyways, Mr. Wolf thought. Pigs liked pigsties, and that was a known fact. If this was not a well-known law office, I would not trust these pigs to defend me, he said to himself.

Mr. Wolf stumbled several times as he tried to make his way through the mess. At one point, he skidded on a banana peel, and had to grab a wall to steady himself. The receptionist mouthed a quick apology. Inwardly Mr. Wolf was fuming despite the apology since the receptionist had not had the courtesy to tell him to be careful. Mr. Wolf tried to calm his temper before he spoke to the lawyer. The next door to the right of the reception area was Counsel Boar's office, and the receptionist knocked loudly before entering.

"Come in," Counsel Boar oinked loudly. The receptionist opened the door to an even messier office space. The lawyer sat buried behind a mountain of files. He was dressed in a crisp white long-sleeved shirt with a green tie as his fuchsia jacket hugged the back of his long burgundy leather chair. He was peering so intently at a stack of files immediately in front of him that he did not acknowledge Mr. Wolf upon his entry. The lawyer was quite a heavyset pig whose girth showed his overindulgence in food. Counsel Boar had a silver pair of glasses perched on his snout that shaded his weary eyes from overly bright glares of light.

"How can I help you, Mr. Wolf?" Counsel Boar asked suddenly in a jovial voice without looking up from his files. Mr. Wolf cleared his throat quite nervously and said a bit timidly, "I want to clear my name, sir."

"From what or whom?" asked Counsel Boar, finally looking up from a manila folder.

"Well, you know the story," Mr. Wolf said, looking somewhat nervous as he cushioned his rear in a leather seat across from the lawyer. Mr. Wolf realized, not for the first time, that he was putting his fate in the hooves of a pig. He wondered again maybe for the millionth time whether it was wise to seek representation from a pig. It was these very same pigs who had gotten him into trouble, but Counsel Boar came highly recommended from both pigs and wolves alike, thought Mr. Wolf as he stared directly at the portly pig.

"What story are you referring to, Mr. Wolf?" asked Counsel Boar quite curiously.

"The story of The Three Little Pigs," said Mr. Wolf very softly.

"Oh that story!" Counsel Boar exclaimed excitedly.

"I was just a piglet when that occurred." Counsel Boar laughed to himself as he recollected what he knew about the story of The Three Little Pigs. His recollections of the story did not make Mr. Wolf look very good. Becoming serious, Counsel Boar looked at Mr. Wolf and in a no-nonsense voice asked, "But that was so long ago; why didn't you clear your name then?" Counsel Boar gave Mr. Wolf a long penetrating stare as he waited for his answer.

"Well, initially, I thought it was cool to have the reputation of the 'big bad wolf,' said Mr. Wolf quietly.

CHAPTER THREE

"So what changed?" Counsel Boar asked incredulously.

"I am now older and wiser," replied Mr. Wolf. "Furthermore, I did not do what those pigs said I did. I am the long-suffering victim in this tall tale, plain and simple."

"You did not?" Counsel Boar asked clearly in disbelief.

"I did not do those things," whispered Mr. Wolf, already tired of explaining himself. Counsel Boar noted the dejected look on Mr. Wolf's face and quickly remembered his role as an attorney. He had a legal duty to represent his clients zealously, and he did not want to lose a potential client based on preconceived notions and prejudices. He had to appear impartial so Mr. Wolf would feel comfortable with him and hire him as his attorney.

"So what exactly happened on the day in question, Mr. Wolf?" Counsel Boar asked, curious to hear Mr. Wolf's side of the story. Over the next two hours, Mr. Wolf proceeded to fill Counsel Boar in on his account of what happened so many years ago. Counsel Boar listened intently, occasionally questioning Mr. Wolf while his conservatively dressed law assistant in a blue-collared shirt and navy-blue pencil skirt took copious notes without uttering a solitary word. Occasionally she had to offer some tissue to Mr. Wolf to wipe away tears as he recounted his story. Returning to her notes, the pig seemed almost robotic as her pen moved from left to right on the yellow legal pad, leaving endless eight-by-eleven pages filled with a sea of words in its wake. After listening to Mr. Wolf's version of the story, Counsel Boar glanced at the round-faced clock across from his desk and saw he had to conclude his consultation with Mr. Wolf. For lawyers, time was money and more clients meant more money. He checked his red heavily penciled appointment book and noted he had several more clients to see before he left the office for the day.

"I think you have a very good case because all we have so far is a one-sided story told by The Three Pigs," Counsel Boar said.

"Mr. Wolf, I believe you would make a credible witness. Therefore I would be honored to be your attorney."

Mr. Wolf was excited that Counsel Boar had decided to take the case. Mr. Wolf jumped up quite animatedly and tried to do a dance in

Counsel Boar's office, but because of his advanced age and bad leg, it looked more as if he was just stumbling around drunken by the bitter-sweet taste of a possible vindication.

"Don't get so excited, Mr. Wolf. We have a long uphill battle ahead of us," said Counsel Boar, hating to have to put a damper on Mr. Wolf's exuberance.

"Wait till I tell Mrs. Wolf that your law office has decided to take my case," Mr. Wolf said. "She will be so surprised."

"Why?" Counsel Boar asked.

"Well, she didn't think you would," said Mr. Wolf sheepishly.

"Why?" asked Counsel Boar, looking amused.

"She didn't think you would, that's all," said Mr. Wolf, becoming quite embarrassed at this line of questioning.

"Tell her not all pigs are the same," said Counsel Boar with a chuckle, showing Mr. Wolf he was not the least bit offended.

After Mr. Wolf left, Counsel Boar sat in his cluttered office and reflected on his decision to represent Mr. Wolf, a notorious villain, in the pig community. He knew there would be consequences for taking the case, but he loved a good fight. He also thought it was time he helped set the record straight. Counsel Boar knew he was getting older, and he wanted to retire early, but he needed one last big win. He lay back in his reclining chair with his head resting on the back of his hooves and thought of the money he would make off this case. Counsel Boar stared at the retainer agreement Mr. Wolf had just signed signifying that Counsel Boar would be entitled to at least thirty-three percent of whatever Mr. Wolf won in court. This could be in the millions if he played his cards right. Counsel Boar was in hog heaven.

This case could allow Counsel Boar to retire in style. Instantly, his imagination conjured up a remote part of the world with lots of sun-shine, white sandy beaches, and the bluest, clearest water. He closed his eyes as if to savor the image of the most exotic mud baths while soaking up the sun and drinking lots of coconut water. He could fish, or golf, or idle the day away as he pleased. Counsel Boar thought about all the publicity he would get: free press conferences, TV appearances, and most of all the envy and respect of the legal community.

Thus far, Counsel Boar had a mixed reputation in the legal community. Most saw him as an ambulance chaser just taking any case that came in the door. Many of them scorned him because of the unsavory clients he defended. Here was his chance to prove them wrong. He could make the money while representing a high-profile client. Counsel Boar smiled as he contemplated the strategy he would employ in the case of *Mr. Wolf v. The Three Pigs*. He raised himself up on his hind legs, straightened his tie, and did a piggy jig around his office to the tune of, "*Did You Ever Think You Could Get This Rich?*" It was a song he heard frequently played on a popular oldies station. Counsel Boar laughed and then chided himself; maybe he should not count his check before it cashed.

After composing himself, Counsel Boar called in his paralegal; a gangly pig armed with a legal notepad and a pen, and gave him instructions to begin research on the case. Counsel Boar searched for court cases that were similar to the case of Mr. Wolf. These were cases that would serve as a precedent for any ruling concerning Mr. Wolf's case. Already, several theories were forming in his mind. He just had to figure out what would fly in a town overrun by pigs. Counsel Boar was not sure Mr. Wolf could get a fair trial, but he would do his best since Mr. Wolf's money and Counsel Boar's reputation depended on it.

"You're going out with a bang of a hooray, old boy," Counsel Boar muttered to himself, quite pleased with the day's events. All Counsel Boar had to do now was plan his course of attack on the pigs. He wondered whom The Three Pigs would hire, since countless lawyers would be chomping at the bit to get this case, because of the publicity it would garner. He hummed as he waited for his next appointment with a pig that a fifty-passenger city bus had rear-ended. The pig incurred serious bodily injury and damage to his car. *Yup, this day is shaping up quite interestingly,* Counsel Boar thought as he returned to his previously unattended files.

CHAPTER FOUR

HOMECOMING

Mr. Wolf left Counsel Boar's office highly elated. He felt a confidence he had not felt in years. He held his head high and waived his bushy tail back and forth, as he briskly walked home with renewed vigor. Finally, things were going his way, and he desperately needed to call Mrs. Wolf to share the good news. For the first time in his life, Mr. Wolf wished he had one of those traveling phones his children and grandchildren permanently affixed to their bodies whenever he saw them. They never seemed to put those phones down. They had it when they ate, played, and even when they slept. The phones rang constantly, and when the phones were not ringing or singing, his grandchildren were frantically texting (whatever that meant). After walking for miles, Mr. Wolf spotted a red and white telephone booth equipped with a phone and a small black bench on the outskirts of the city. It was one of the last remaining relics of time past. Mr. Wolf opened the red, square, boxed, glass door, squeezed into the tight space, and inserted the required change into the coin slot. He dialed Mrs. Wolf, wondering with trepidation what type of reaction he would get.

Meanwhile back at home, Mrs. Wolf was curled up on a handmade floral blue and grey hammock as she watched her favorite talk show. The topic was quite interesting, "Finding Your Authentic Self after the Children Have Gone." It is just what I need, Mrs. Wolf thought. Her little wolves were grown and now raising their own little wolves. She was now retired and had many things she could do, according to the expert on *Oprah*. Mrs. Wolf was excited for the first time in a while. She wondered when O would have a show on "Letting Go of the Past." She would definitely have to get Mr. Wolf to watch that, even if she had to tie him to the couch. She chuckled as she remembered why she was home alone. Mr. Wolf had gone to see that Pig attorney—simply chasing an elusive dream, she thought, and Mrs. Wolf was displeased about that. However, she was quite content to have the house to herself since she did not have to listen to Mr. Wolf rattle on about his stupid problem with The Three Pigs.

Mrs. Wolf sighed wearily. She knew Mr. Wolf would be so disappointed when that Pig attorney refused to take his case, but at least it would be the end of this nonsense, she rationalized. As a result, she would no longer have to listen to his continual chatter, "The Three Little Pigs this, and The Three Little Pigs that." The shrill ringing of the black rotary phone plastered to the kitchen wall abruptly interrupted Mrs. Wolf's rambling thoughts.

Mrs. Wolf glanced at the clock, wondering who was calling her during her favorite show. Mrs. Wolf grabbed the phone and yelled loudly into the receiver, "Hello!"

"The pig took the case," yelled Mr. Wolf quite loudly through the phone, almost shattering Mrs. Wolf's eardrum. Mrs. Wolf was speechless, as she could not believe her ears. She stared at the phone, not knowing quite how to respond.

"The pig took the case?" she whispered softly.

What is this world coming to? Now I will never hear the end of this case, thought Mrs. Wolf as she sighed wearily.

"Did you hear me, Mrs. Wolf?" "I told you the pig would take the case," Mr. Wolf said with exuberance.

"Yes, I heard you," she replied in disbelief. "Get home safe." Then she hung up the phone. Mrs. Wolf immediately felt faint, and she could feel an instant headache coming on. *This is becoming a nightmare*, she thought. She needed to lie down because the room suddenly seemed to be spinning, and it had gotten decidedly hotter. She crawled to her bedroom, her legs somewhat protected from the hard floor by her pink flannel pajamas. Mrs. Wolf hoped she would soon wake up from this terrible nightmare.

Mr. Wolf, on the other end of the phone sighed ruefully; and hoped Mrs. Wolf would recover from her shock. He smiled quite happily, and nothing could bring his spirits down, not even Mrs. Wolf. He quickly hung up the phone and began his journey home, this time ignoring the many stares and jeers the pigs were sending his way.

CHAPTER FIVE

SERVICE OF PROCESS

Several weeks later Counsel Boar went to file Mr. Wolf's complaint with the county clerk in the basement of the courthouse in Maplewood. He handed the required fee to the clerk, who in turn gave Counsel Boar an index number. This number would stay with the case until the end to help identify it for any of the parties involved. The clerk also gave Counsel Boar a copy of the summons and complaint. The town process server would be responsible for serving The Three Pigs with the legal paperwork. The court papers, clearly marked SUMMONS AND COMPLAINT, outlined the details of the case against The Three Pigs. The summons also firmly ordered The Three Pigs to answer within a specified period of time. The complaint was captioned *Mr. Wolf v. The Three Pigs*. The lawsuit named Mr. Wolf as the plaintiff, since he had brought the lawsuit. The complaint named The Three Pigs as the defendants, since Mr. Wolf was suing them. The court papers also stated that the location of the case would be Maplewood Civil Part. Furthermore, Mr. Wolf was suing the pigs for $20,000,000 in damages.

Counsel Boar perused the contents of the service papers that read:

COURT OF MAPLEWOOD
CIVIL COURT

---x

MR. WOLF

            Plaintiff,

Vs.

                    Index Number: 12345

BRICK HOUSE PIG
STRAW HOUSE PIG   **VERIFIED COMPLAINT**
STICK HOUSE PIG

            Defendants.

---x

Plaintiff, resident of the woods on the outskirts of Maplewood, by his attorney, Counsel Boar, complaining of the Defendant(s), alleges as follows: The Defendants, Brick House Pig, Stick House Pig, and Straw House Pig are siblings residing within the jurisdiction of Maplewood.

AS AND FOR A FIRST CAUSE OF ACTION
ON BEHALF OF MR. WOLF
<u>DEFAMATION</u>

1.   At all times hereinafter-mentioned Plaintiff, Mr. Wolf, was a resident of the woods on the outskirts of Maplewood.

2.   At all times hereinafter-mentioned Defendants, Brick House Pig, Stick House Pig, and Straw House Pig were residents of the City of Maplewood.

3.   On or about 15th day of Said Year at approximately 12:00 p.m. while inside the jurisdiction of Maplewood Defendants, The Three Pigs, did jointly and/or severally, intentionally defame Mr. Wolf by spreading rumors concerning Plaintiff, Mr. Wolf's, character making him out to be a carnivorous beast who attacked them without provocation.

4.   On or about the date indicated Defendants, The Three Pigs, claimed falsely that Mr. Wolf tried to harm them.

5.   That since the intentional acts complained of Plaintiff, Mr. Wolf, has suffered damage to his reputation, ability to pursue professional endeavors, and has been denied employment and therefore obligated to and necessarily did engage in menial jobs that were insufficient to support his family.

6.   That since the intentional acts complained of Plaintiff, Mr. Wolf, has suffered monetary damage as he has lost several professional opportunities that would have resulted in diverse sums of money as such he has had to request public assistance from the City of Maplewood and rely on whatever money his wife, Mrs. Wolf, earns.

7.   The statements made by Defendants, The Three Pigs, were slurs on Mr. Wolf's character and resulted in damage to, The Plaintiff, Mr. Wolf's reputation in the community in that: whenever Mr. Wolf encounters pigs within Maplewood they often flee in horror or mock and make fun of him.

8.   The slanderous statements made by The Three Pigs damaged Mr. Wolf's ability to move into reputable and desirable neighborhoods due to his *"bad reputation."* Thereby, The Three Pig's actions resulted in Mr. Wolf having to reside in the woods isolated from most of society thus causing him to live as a recluse for many years

due to embarrassment and mainstream society's refusal to accept his integration into their community.

AS AND FOR A SECOND CAUSE OF ACTION ON BEHALF OF MR. WOLF OF EXTREME EMOTIONAL DISTRESS

9.   Defendants, The Three Pigs, intentionally and deliberately inflicted emotional distress on the Plaintiff, Mr. Wolf.

10.   As a result of Defendants, The Three Pigs,' extreme and outrageous conduct, Mr. Wolf continues to suffer from sleep deprivation, and has been unable to obtain a full night's sleep.

11.   As a result of Defendants, The Three Pigs,' outrageous conduct, Mr. Wolf has suffered and will continue to suffer mental pain and anguish, severe emotional trauma, embarrassment, and humiliation.

WHEREFORE, the Plaintiff demands judgment against the Defendants: on the first and second causes of action on behalf of Plaintiff, Mr. Wolf, in the amount of 20,000,000 million dollars; together with the costs and disbursements of this action and for such other and further relief as to this court may deem just and proper.

Dated: April 28th of This Year

Counsel Boar
Law Offices of HP and HP
By: Counsel Boar
Attorney for Plaintiff

Cc:

Law Offices of Priggly, Priggly and Priggly, Attorneys for Stick House Pig and Brick House Pig. Straw House Pig, Pro Se Defendant.

Mr. Wolf, being first duly sworn, affirms that he has read the foregoing complaint and that he knows the content thereof, and that the same is true, except those matters therein stated to be upon information and belief, and as to those matters, he believe to be true.

Mr. Wolf

_____

Plaintiff

Sworn and subscribed before me this 30th day of April This year

Notary Public, John Brown, Maplewood

My commission expires December 28th, of Next Year

Court Papers Served Inc. sent Guinea Pig, one of Maplewoods' youngest process servers, to serve The Three Pigs notice of the impending court case. He was a small, slender, quick-witted fellow who had been with the company over a year, working to pay his tuition at Maplewood Community College. He skillfully and furiously pedaled his fancy old bicycle down Maple Lane, bent on completing the mission at hand. As Guinea Pig weaved in and out of traffic, the blustery wind blew back strands of his stringy black and green streaked hair that escaped from the red baseball cap he wore with the company's logo and name. His messenger bag tightly packed with legal papers for a number of unlucky recipients. Today he slung it carefully across his right shoulder, seemingly bent on protecting his precious cargo. The first pig he decided to serve was the pig that used to live in the brick house.

The Brick House Pig, the oldest of The Three Pigs, had been somewhat interesting to serve. Her neighborhood was in a rather exclusive section of Maplewood. It stood a few miles from the center of town and known for its manicured lawns and opulent homes. A magnificent wrought iron black gate surrounded Brick House Pig's residence. It was well secured, and guarded by a rather fierce-looking middle-aged, brown-faced pit bull that constantly paced back and forth with a walkie-talkie in his paws. He was dressed in a grey blazer, white cotton shirt, a blue tie, and white seamed pants.

Guinea Pig chained his bicycle to a fence and walked up to the gate serving as a barrier between the Brick House Pig's residence and outsiders. Guinea Pig was used to dealing with all types of delicate situations, so he gave the Pit Bull a cheerful greeting and stated the nature of his business. The Pit Bull did not utter a word. Instead, he walked a few feet away and exchanged words with someone via his walkie-talkie. Suddenly, Guinea Pig watched the towering gates slowly slide open.

The Pit Bull never cracked a smile as he ushered Guinea Pig through the gates. He looked Guinea Pig up and down before patting him down for any dangerous weapons. The Pit Bull looked feral as he eyed Guinea Pig with his coal black eyes. Guinea Pig smiled to himself, since the only dangerous weapon he ever carried were the court papers he was about to serve on the owner of the property. The Pit Bull, noting Guinea Pig's smile, growled as he kept a watchful eye on him. At that moment, a timid-looking white-faced rabbit darted from behind a clump of scarlet rosebushes and politely beckoned Guinea Pig to follow her.

The white rabbit escorted Guinea Pig through the grounds via a cobblestone walkway that led to the black French double doors of the huge well-kept house. Guinea Pig looked on quite amused as the rabbit awkwardly smoothed the folds of her ill-fitting black and white uniform that identified her as the help. As they turned the corner, the sight of expansive green landscaping, punctuated with well-pruned pine trees that seemed to reach their lofty branches to the heavens, greeted Guinea Pig. Several tall fountains located throughout the grounds indiscriminately spewed water from large spouts over the roving landscape. In the center of this splendor was an antique-white three-story mansion detailed with two luminous Roman pillars and a balcony anchored on the second story. A long, paved, black driveway partially occupied by a grey four-door Bentley, and two larger-than-life bronze-plated lion statues, which appeared to stand guard at each side of the gold-plated door.

The stocky housecleaner led Guinea Pig toward the black French doors. As she pushed open the door, Guinea Pig saw a voluptuous pig with platinum-blonde hair tied back with a scarf. She was standing in the center of a breathtaking sparkling-white foyer complete with ceiling-high windows draped in crimson satin curtains. Guinea Pig immediately surmised her to be Brick House Pig. She was elegantly coiffed in a brown wool two-piece pantsuit with a cream turtleneck blouse, complemented by three layers of pearls that cascaded almost down to her waist. Two rail-thin deeply tanned female teenage pigs dressed in identical tennis attire with platinum-blonde hair wound tightly into ponytails stood on either side of the expensively clad pig. The older female pig, noting Guinea Pig's arrival, whispered something to the girls that sent them scurrying off in the direction of the black spiral staircase. Both raced noisily to the top of the dozen or more steps before disappearing from sight.

The house-cleaner looked at the pig nervously before saying, "Missus, he is here on an urgent matter," pointing to Guinea Pig accusingly. The pig looked at the frazzled house-cleaner and said, "That will be all," dismissing the rabbit. She scurried out of the room, closing the kitchen door behind her. She pressed her big white ears to the door, eager to hear what was happening to her employer. She hoped it would not affect her job because things had been tense between the missus and mister in the past months due to the bad economy. The house-cleaner prayed whatever was happening between the missus and that Guinea Pig would not take long since she had a load of laundry to do for those two, spoiled, and unmanageable, piglets. Outside the foyer, the voluptuous pig fixed her disapproving gaze on Guinea Pig as she noted his uniform.

"How may I help you?" she asked in a clipped tone.

"I have papers to serve you, Mrs. Brick House Pig," said Guinea Pig as he wiped his sweaty paws on his pants. He reached into his red bag before pushing the complaint and summons toward Brick House Pig. She grimaced and wrinkled her nose in distaste before stretching her hoof reluctantly to receive the papers.

"Compliments of Mr. Wolf, madam, I hope you have a nice day!" said Guinea Pig, tipping his hat as he raced out of Brick House Pig's residence, not sparing her another glance. He sped through the grounds at lightning speed, only slowing as he neared the Pit Bull.

"Have a good day, sir," he muttered as the Pit Bull slid open the gate while eyeing Guinea Pig suspiciously. Guinea Pig stopped when he neared his bicycle, reached into his bag, and took out the affidavit of service. The affidavit of service listed the time Guinea Pig had served Brick House Pig, her description, and her address. Guinea Pig would have to go through this process two more times with the two other pigs.

He unlocked his bike and pedaled away, waving at Pit Bull, with a silly grin on his face. He just loved sticking it to these pigs. He rushed off to find the pig that lived in the stick house.

Stick House Pig lived high above the city in an upscale thirty-story, pebbled stone, high-rise building located in the heart of the upper east side of the City of Maplewood. Her residence was one of the few buildings in the exclusive section of Maplewood that had a rooftop pool. Her floor to ceiling windows stood naked in the atmosphere as streams of golden sunlight flooded the 2,100-square-foot space living quarters. Puffs of gentle autumn breeze drifted through all three bedrooms, 3.5 bathrooms featuring marble baths, and a kitchen with an island and granite countertops. Down the many stories below, it was business as usual in the neighborhood. The street was bustling with harried-looking nannies ushering their wayward charges to various museums and play dates. Sharply dressed CEOs in Armani attire peered intently at the morning papers and occasionally glanced impatiently at their watches. They waited for their drivers who maneuvered their way through the almost snail-like traffic to their destinations. Bored young housewives stood around on every corner of the building. Every morning they would quickly wave off their offspring to caretakers who scarcely had time to enter the building when the mother pigs would hand them over to the caretakers with not even so much as a wave. Breathing sighs of relief, the housewives sauntered back to bed or to the salons to get their full body makeovers, saunas, hairstyling, manicures, and pedicures. Many of them were trophy wives of older harried spouses who expected them to appear picture perfect as complements to their disposable assets of their ever-growing portfolios. Still others spent their days bossing the help around to ensure that their residential spaces were spotless. Their favorite pastime was meeting the crew for lunch to catch up on the neighborhood gossip. Others spent the time shopping for designer brands in expensive boutiques.

Guinea Pig paused for a moment to take it all in before persuading the door attendant to lure Stick House Pig to the front of the building. The door attendant was quite cooperative since he was still smarting from not receiving a gratuity from Stick House Pig from the last holiday. He summoned Stick House Pig to the lobby under the pretense of receiving a delivery. Stick House Pig received the call from the lobby and hurriedly tossed on some clothes. Once fully clad in her purple Juicy Couture sweat suit and Jimmy Choo sandals, she glanced appreciatively around her luxurious apartment as if seeing it for the first time. The walls painted in cool pastel shades displayed several expensive paintings. The paintings hung at strategic angles. Above the fireplace, family portraits reminded her of earlier times when she had not a care in the world and life was oh so simple. Positioned on the mantelpiece was an exotic painting she had posed for at age twenty-one when she had vacationed in Paris with her ex-husband. *I was stunningly beautiful then,* she thought.

Stick House Pig sighed ruefully before fixing her gaze on her prized portrait of the pig's version of the *Mona Lisa* that hung in the center of the foyer. She had purchased it at an auction, and she hoped to sell it later for a tidy sum when the price appreciated. The shiny white marble floors sparkled like clear crystal and formed an elegant backdrop for the Victorian antique furniture she purchased at the estate sale of a deceased Maplewood socialite. As she trotted toward the door, she was careful not to leave any marks on the black and white Persian rug that rolled from the front door to the end of the foyer. Before exiting the apartment, she smiled at her good fortune and paused shortly before the large wall mirror by the door to pat a few stray strands of hair into place.

Stick House Pig hurried to the lobby and headed toward the black glossy front desk to speak to the receptionist, but he was nowhere in sight. She wondered which of her many packages had arrived, but in her eagerness, she failed to notice the rather amused look of the door attendant when he told her the package was outside. Stick House Pig stepped outside the glass revolving door, yet she did not see any signs of a delivery truck. Instead, Guinea Pig jumped out of the hedges, shoved some papers at her, and yelled, "This is for you, Stick House Pig; you have been served compliments of Mr. Wolf. See you in court."

Guinea Pig grabbed his bicycle and skillfully hopped on before she could respond. Stick House Pig glared at Guinea Pig in disbelief, but he simply smirked at her before cycling away. He stopped a block away and filled out the Affidavit of Service.

"So far, so good," he whispered to himself.

"It's now time to get the Straw House Pig."

Stick House Pig had quickly snatched the papers from Guinea Pig as she scanned the grounds for any onlookers. She could not afford for any of her neighbors to witness this, and she was glad most of them were already at work for the day. Stick House Pig was glad she had taken the day off from her office job, so no one would be privy to her humiliation. The majority of them, like the uppity Mrs. Winkle, were trust fund babies, and they already thought she did not fit into their upper-crust neighborhood since their money stretched several generations back.

"It is already embarrassing that this nosy doorman, a notorious gossip, is a witness to my humiliation," she said to herself.

"I suspect that this would not be happening if I had gifted him some money during the holidays. I guess the saying is true that no deed goes unpunished."

She hurried into the building, partially concealing the papers inside her jacket as she rushed for the elevator and almost slipped. She pressed the elevator button for up, clearly ignoring the hovering door attendant who asked with a barely disguised sneer, "Is everything OK?"

Stick House Pig ignored him and slid into the elevator, relieved it was empty. The elevator door closed to the hysterical laughter of the door attendant, who by this time was rolling around on the red-carpeted floor, glad that the fake uppity pig was getting what was coming to her.

After she read them, Stick House Pig realized her mistake in snatching the papers. It stated Mr. Wolf was suing her for millions of dollars. It was the past coming back to haunt her. Stick House Pig shrieked, "Where am I going to get millions of dollars? I cannot even count all those zeros, much less pay that sum. As it is, I can barely keep a roof over our head living in the expensive City of Maplewood with the many gourmet shops, the expensive gym membership I rarely use, the exclusive country club membership, my daughter's tuition, and my insatiable appetite for eating at fancy, expensive, five-star restaurants almost every night. But as they say, location, location, location, and Maplewood allows me the opportunity to mingle with the wealthy."

When she returned to her apartment, she sat on her sofa and thought for a while, "*I guess I have to stay put if I want to keep up with big sister. She is the intelligent and wealthy one. I refuse to live like a pauper,*" she finally said to herself before trotting to the bathroom to take a shower. A few moments later, Stick House Pig's socialite daughter Olivia sauntered into the apartment, her hair a streaming mass of manufactured platinum curls, as she had just come back from the hair salon. The cost of her hair had left a sizable dent on her mother's American Express card; however, it was worth it, since she wanted all eyes on her when she sashayed into the school dance later that night at the exclusive school her mother forced her to attend.

Olivia's waif-like lower body hugged strategically lined jeans that cost hundreds of dollars, while her upper body was snuggled in a cashmere sweater, the price of which could feed a family of four for a month. Olivia was quite startled as she heard her mother's high-pitched voice using words not suitable for polite company. She wondered what had gotten her mother so riled up, but she quickly forgot about her mother as her cell phone rang and she became engaged in the latest gossip with her schoolmate.

After serving court papers on Stick House Pig, Guinea Pig, decked out in red skinny jeans and a matching colored jacket, with the words **Court Papers Served Inc.**, hurried to find the Straw House Pig. Guinea Pig had to make three attempts, as required by law, before he could finally serve the pig that had lived in the straw house. The first time, he went to her house early in the morning. Guinea Pig was sure the pig had been home.

"I heard her heavy breathing as she hid behind her front door," he told one of his colleagues on the phone. "I even saw her crusty painted hoof under the door, but she did not respond to my repeated knocks. Maybe her sisters told her about the summons she was about to receive."

The second time, Guinea Pig returned to Straw House Pig's house in the afternoon and finally again in the evening. This time Mr. Guinea Pig was about to nail the court papers to the door of the house when he saw her strolling listlessly down the lane as if she had no set destination. Straw House Pig was dressed in a patchwork jeans jacket, overly tight pink T-shirt, a white and red plaid pleated skirt, polka dot stockings, and worn black combat boots that reached up to her knees. She carried a rather large white paper bag stuffed with goodies purchased at Mickey Slop, a popular burger place in town.

"Let me get outta here; there goes that annoying Guinea Pig again. What does he want with me?" Straw House Pig asked, hurrying away in the other direction.

"I heard he's looking for me, and I know he is up to no good." Her dyed red ringlets flopped back and forth in the wind as she ran, so Guinea Pig chased her down the road.

"This is a bit unorthodox, but this fat pig is not getting away today," said Guinea Pig. "My boss at Court Papers Served, Inc. will be highly upset if I do not serve these papers. Furthermore, I have a reputation to uphold."

Straw House Pig no longer resembled a little pig since she had gained so much weight by eating everything in sight. "Go away, you idiot, and let me be," she shouted breathlessly as Guinea Pig pursued her. He was smaller and faster, and he quickly caught up with her. She shoved Guinea Pig as she tried to get away. The Mickey Slop burgers, curly fries, and shakes flew into the air and landed on the black pavement. The strawberry shake made a big splatter on the sidewalk and the curly fries littered the streets haphazardly. The burgers lost their tidy order, landing in various sections of the street. A hungry dog passing by rushed to eat up the goodies, but Straw House Pig shooed him away and tried to salvage what she could of the remains of her dinner, all the time cursing at Mr. Guinea Pig.

"You smelly old runt, look what you did! You made me lose my supper, and you are going to pay." Mr. Guinea Pig, seeing that Straw House Pig was momentarily distracted, tried to shove the papers in her hoof. She kicked him on the shin as she tried to run faster than him.

"Ouch! You slob of a pig," yelled Mr. Guinea Pig while grabbing his foot in pain. He became agitated and chased Straw House Pig down the tree-lined block of one-story row houses and thrust the court papers full force at her once again. The ruckus attracted a group of onlookers who gathered to see who would win the battle of the wills.

"Whoop that guinea pig!" someone shouted.

"Stomp on his corn toe, then make mince pork chops out of him!" shouted another as they clapped and cheered on Straw House Pig.

"Look at what you did to my clean jacket, you moron! It's messed up with ketchup and strawberry shake," shouted Straw House Pig breathlessly. "I have no business with you, and I will not take those papers."

"Oh yes, you will take the papers; no way are you going to ruin my reputation," he replied, shoving the papers at her.

"Really! Really! Paperboy let us see about that. You can speak to the hoof, you dumb fool!" she replied, thrusting her right front hoof in his face as she turned her back on Guinea Pig and hurried home.

Guinea Pig shook his head thinking, *just like a pig*, before speeding ahead and beating Straw House Pig to her front door. He dropped the summons right in front of her door. As he bicycled away, Mr. Guinea Pig glanced back at Straw House Pig and said quietly, with a smirk on his face, "You have been served." The look on Straw House Pig's face was priceless, but Mr. Guinea Pig was quite satisfied that he had fulfilled his legal duty.

As Mr. Guinea Pig headed down the lane, Straw House Pig yelled at the top of her lungs at him, "Traitor! You're nothing but a fake pig anyway."

Mr. Guinea Pig had heard this claim so many times before, so he was unaffected by her taunts. He was just relieved he had finally cornered the pig and served her the papers. He did not care what the other pigs in town thought about him anyway, since most of them, like the fat pig, had never considered him a real pig. The Guinea pig, to most pigs, was a pig in name only.

CHAPTER SIX

THE THREE PIGS' REACTION

ach of The Three Pigs reacted quite differently to the court papers. Brick House Pig was incensed when she received the court papers from Mr. Guinea Pig. She thought she had lived down the notoriety of this whole story with the wolf. Now many years later, when it appeared the incident was in the distant past, it was coming back to haunt her. Brick House Pig's life was comfortable just the way it was. She had made several millions in the real estate market by investing her earnings from writing the story of <u>The Three Little Pigs</u> and selling it to publishers and tabloids. She had written the story via a ghostwriter so many years ago when she was young and inexperienced. Now she was more sophisticated and married to old money. She did not need or want the publicity that would come with this case. She clearly remembered all the notoriety she had received from the case with the wolf, and she did not want a repeat of the experience.

Brick House Pig fumed as she thought about who was responsible for this mess. She was so upset that she had to sit down before trying to contact an attorney. While Brick House Pig had a real estate attorney on retainer, she had to find an attorney that specialized in defamation. Brick House Pig still could not believe the evil old wolf was suing her. He surely had some nerve suing his victims. *My husband the real estate mogul will have a fit when he hears about this*, she thought. He was already having his own issues trying to recover from the housing loan fiasco, and he did not need another problem on his hands. She sat on the couch, glanced through the complaint and summons for a while with her chin cupped in her front hooves, and then softly whispered, "What a conundrum." It immediately dawned on Brick House Pig what attorney she would call. This attorney was quite reputable and famous. She was from the Law Firm of Priggly, Priggly, and Priggly-one of the oldest international firms in town. The founding pigs had started the firm in England and had opened branches all over the world. She knew Ms. Priggly was quite selective in taking on clients, so she would probably have to call in a few favors to be able to retain the law firm's services. Brick House Pig sighed as she lightly touched her expensively done platinum blond hair. It was time to get the roots done again, she mused wearily.

Brick House Pig was startled when the phone in her bedroom rang loudly. She rushed over to pick it up and said, "Hello, how can I help you?" into the receiver.

"It's me, sister," said the voice from the other end.

"Oh, it is you," replied Brick House Pig. "What is the matter?"

"Did that Guinea Pig serve you some court papers?" Stick House Pig asked.

"Yes, he did," replied Brick House Pig with a loud sigh.

"You are the calm and sensible one," Stick House Pig said. "So what are we going to do?"

"Let me think about it, and I will call you back," Brick House Pig replied.

Stick House Pig did not need this aggravation, and she shuddered at the thought of the cost she would incur acquiring legal representation. She thought about the designer brands like Bashy, Prada, and Gucci that lined her closets. Spring was not far away, and she needed to update her wardrobe. This court case could do some serious damage to her finances and consequently her wardrobe. This would definitely not do, so she had some serious thinking to do. Stick House Pig also wanted to get to the culprit in this fiasco, and she knew this had to be the doings of her little sister, Straw House Pig. She was the only person Stick House Pig knew who could get them into this type of drama. Straw House Pig was the youngest and the spoiled one, but her many schemes had been the bane of their existence. This time, however, she had had enough. Stick House Pig went back inside to place a phone call to her older sister, Brick House Pig. She could already feel the onset of a stress headache. *This day is definitely going from bad to worse, and Brick House Pig needs to come up with a way to make this lawsuit go away*, Stick House Pig thought as she redialed her older sister. Brick House Pig would probably be irritated to hear from her again so soon, but "Isn't this what big sisters are for?" Stick House Pig wondered aloud, wishing she could just crawl back under her covers and wish the tragedy that was her life away.

"That Guinea Pig has nothing on me. I did not even touch those papers, so I will not have to go to court," Straw House Pig boasted to her friend. They had dropped by the courthouse to see what was going on because of the excitement surrounding the lawsuit.

A lawyer, who was in earshot of this conversation, walked over to Straw House Pig and replied, "Yes, you will have to go to court since you were given notice of the lawsuit by virtue of the summons even if you did not take it in your hoof."

Straw House Pig looked at her as if she was going to faint and started to cry hysterically. She knew her sisters blamed her for this whole court fiasco. Hours later, at home, when Straw House Pig recalled the conversation, she raced to get some food from the refrigerator. She was depressed, so she ate. Straw House Pig's sisters always called her an emotional eater, but she did not care. Eating comfort food right now was the only way to deal with this lawsuit problem.

Straw House Pig could not even afford to hire her own lawyer. After careful consideration, she realized she simply could not pay the exorbitant prices they were charging. Some lawyers quoted prices such as three hundred dollars an hour. This got Straw House Pig thinking.

If only I had listened to Mother and stayed in school, I could have been a lawyer, she said to herself. I would be the one charging clients hundreds of dollars an hour and living in one of those fancy buildings with a door attendant right in the heart of the city and access to the park. This ridiculous idea made her laugh since no one thought she was very bright. Lawyers had to be bright considering they had to do all those years of schooling. Straw House Pig knew she did not have the discipline or the brains for that kind of education.

Throughout her school years, the other pigs called Straw House Pig all sorts of unflattering names such as dimwit, dummy, silly, and clueless, but the most degrading was bush pig. This abuse permanently seared her memory. Straw House Pig gazed in the distance as the painful taunts at recess again rang in her ears: "bush pig, bush pig, in your corner," or "bush pig, hears our laughter," and "bush pig, you better scatter." As she reflected on her sad past, the taunts at lunchtime in the piggy school-yard still rang in her ears as if it were yesterday. Her cruel classmates made fun of her inability to comprehend even simple instructions, her homemade hand-me-down clothes from her two older sisters, and the fact that she was so different from her sisters. Many days Straw House Pig fought the pigs that cornered her on the playground and chanted the bush pig song. The unyielding teasing had not stopped, no matter how many times she had transferred schools. The bitter part about the whole saga was that she had stood alone against her tormentors; her friends were few, and no one came to her aid, not even her older sisters.

Her two older sisters had not been much better than the other pigs at school. They had also teased her mercilessly and called her hurtful names. *Why are they so mean to me? I am their baby sister, for crying out loud,* Straw House Pig thought. Tears rolled down her cheeks, and she gave out a deep guttural grunt. Furthermore, her sister, Brick House Pig, was Mother Pig's favorite. She was the brightest of The Three Pigs, and everyone always remarked that Brick House Pig was so smart since she scored A's in all her subjects and had won the National Spelling Bee five years in a row. Stick House Pig was the beautiful one with her petite fig-ure, thick bouncy hair, and uppity airs. Unfortunately, for Straw House

Pig, she was pegged the troubled one; in fact, she never felt loved or accepted, but rather a misfit.

Straw House Pig had dropped out of high school. Dropping out of school had been the beginning of her problems. While she had made some money from the story of The Three Little Pigs, her sisters had made millions of dollars more because they had negotiated better deals than she had. Furthermore, she had squandered all her money on the many get-rich schemes she had seen advertised on the television in the early-morning hours. Losing the bulk of her money in a pyramid scheme was the worst financial disaster that Straw House Pig had experienced.

Straw House Pig was now forced to work minimum wage jobs that could barely pay her expenses. Her one-room studio looked haphazardly decorated, with shocking pink and sunflower yellow wallpaper. The headboard to her full-size bed lay flat on the floor; soiled sheets and pillows neglected in a crumpled heap on one corner of the raggedy mattress while her clothes were scattered around the room. Some of her boots lay bundled up with dirty jeans still tucked inside. Tons of old newspapers, lottery tickets, magazines, DVDs, CDs, and broken CD cases littered the walkway. A few weeks ago, Straw House Pig had even slipped on a broken CD cover and sprained her ankle, yet she still appeared incapable of cleaning up her own mess. Straw House Pig was struggling financially and in need of a lawyer, especially since the legal jargon in the court papers the stupid Guinea Pig had given her seemed quite complex. What was she to do? After speaking to her sisters, Straw House Pig cried even more. Both her sisters had told her she would have to fend for herself in this case with the wolf, since they were tired of cleaning up her messes. Her sisters, Brick House Pig and Stick House Pig, always felt that she ran mindlessly into trouble. Straw House Pig could almost hear her two sisters talking about her and describing her as the silly one. "Ugh," she said, "can life get any worse?" She just had to figure a way out of this predicament.

Just then, the telephone resting on the kitchen table rang. It was her best friend Cindy. Straw House Pig, who was quite frustrated, began to tell Cindy what had transpired the last couple of days.

"I wish that old wolf had just died in the boiling pot of water."

"How come he did not?" asked Cindy curiously between bites of a succulent apple, although quite familiar with the story of Mr. Wolf.

"Because we did not lock the lid on the stupid pot, that's why!" yelled Straw House Pig, jumping up and down as the week-old dirty dishes in the sink and the feeble table in the kitchen shook violently.

"If we had, that darn wolf would have been dead meat. I still don't know how that dumb wolf got away, since Brick House Pig said she had locked all the doors and windows. I just want to know why that old coot is still bothering me."

Straw House Pig continued her angry rant into the phone. She did not give Cindy a chance to get in a word edgewise. Cindy, a notorious gossip, quickly hung up the phone, eager to get away from Straw House Pig. *This is shaping up to be one interesting day*, she thought. Cindy's phone remained quite busy that day as she dialed all the numbers she had programmed into her phone and texted portions of her conversation with Straw House Pig to her friends.

"Let it not be said that I don't have the latest and juiciest gossip," Cindy squealed as she sent an e-mail blast to some of her friends and posted a message on Facebook. She thought, *what are friends for if they could not share juicy gossip with each other*. Besides, it was not as if Straw House Pig did not know she was a gossip, she rationalized.

After the conversation, Straw House Pig grabbed the last half gallon of pistachio-flavored ice cream from the small refrigerator, dug up an old box of Krispy Kreme Donuts from the old bread pan, and started to pig out. A trail of crumbs created a perfect feasting opportunity for a family of mice that nested behind the stove in Straw House Pig's kitchen. The mice went unnoticed as she stuffed her face with her comfort food, as she called it.

Straw House Pig created what was considered a pig parlance, "or a slop." In between grunts of satisfaction, she shoved spoonfuls of ice cream and cookies into her large mouth. She was not concerned that it dripped onto her shirt as she dug furiously into the slop. *I will not be looking in a mirror anytime soon*, she thought. Right now, I just need to feel good, forget about my problems, and worry about the added pounds later, she said to herself as she poked large amounts of food into her mouth.

After Guinea Pig served each of The Three Pigs, he hurried to drop his Affidavit of Service off at the Law Offices of Honest Pig and Honest Pig. Before leaving the papers with the law assistant, Guinea Pig made sure his documents were filled out properly, since his boss would surely have his head if he left out vital information such as the correct address of the pigs, height of the pigs, weight, or any visibly identifying marks located on their bodies. The last time he mistakenly left information out, his boss had threatened to fire him. It would now be Counsel Boar's job to submit the proof of service to the clerk's office in the basement of the Civil Court of Maplewood.

CHAPTER SEVEN

THE CLERK'S OFFICE

Early one morning, Counsel Boar brought the Proof of Service Papers to the clerk's office so he could file them, but he had to join a long line that barely moved. He patiently waited his turn among a long line of lawyers and assistants who were dressed in expensive suits and Rolex watches waiting to file their cases. Every few minutes, several of the lawyers checked their watches and sucked their teeth.

One lawyer from a competing firm standing next to Counsel Boar remarked, "This clerk is so slow on a busy morning such as this. It is such a shame that only one window is open. I have things to do. Do they expect us to spend the whole day here?"

Counsel Boar grunted in agreement, and patiently waited his turn. Time seemed to stand still as the clerk, a sour-faced pig, put *Mr. Wolf v. The Three Pigs* on the calendar. She appeared lifeless and acted as if she did not want employment in the clerk's office.

There are literally thousands of unemployed pigs that would gladly take the place of the sour-faced pig in this tough job market, thought Counsel Boar. As if she could read Counsel Boar's mind, the sour-faced pig gave Counsel Boar an angry glare before handing him the court date, signifying that the case of *Mr. Wolf v. The Three Pigs* had officially begun. Immediately, after handing Counsel Boar the index number, which identified the case, the sour-faced pig put up an eight-by-eleven sign on the clerk's window, which stated, **"Closed, out for lunch. Be back in two hours piggy time."** Counsel Boar looked at the clock prominently displayed in the clerk's office and saw it was only 10:00 a.m. Although it was still quite early in the morning, this was the only clerk's window open, and there was a long line of angry patrons behind him, but the sour-faced pig still left.

"Meet me for lunch at the diner on Heath Street," the clerk cooed into her cell phone as she skipped excitedly out of the office. "We can check out the latest fashions at the Boutique Petit because they have some cool boots on sale. I just want to get away from this stuffy old office with all these lawyers and their legal briefs."

Counsel Boar chuckled and muttered to himself, "And they wonder why people often grumble about those lazy pigs."

After years of practicing law, Counsel Boar knew that coming to the courthouse required both patience and a sense of humor. Luckily, he had an abundance of both. He put his wide-brimmed hat on and walked into the cool air as he exited the court building.

After leaving the courthouse, Counsel Boar called Mr. Wolf and told him the case had officially begun. Mr. Wolf was elated since he would finally have his day in court. He could not wait to share the good news with Mrs. Wolf, who was out looking for bottles to recycle. Mr. Wolf hoped she would finally be happy for him.

Once Guinea Pig served The Three Pigs and the index number became part of the public record, the lawsuit made both national and international news. Hundreds of angry pig supporters surrounded the Law Office of Honest Pig and Honest Pig. Some carried bullhorns and yelled their disdain for wolves at the top of their lungs. Many of the pigs called Counsel Boar a traitor to pigs everywhere. Others claimed that all pigs should boycott his office. The first week of protests led to vandalism at the law offices. Pigs sprayed all the windows with graffiti that said, "**Traitor works here**." Someone sprayed Counsel Boar's black BMW with the words "**TRAITOR ON board**." Someone even posted signs around the town with pictures of Counsel Boar that read, "**Wanted dead before trial**." Many of Counsel Boar's clients refused to come to his office for fear of reprisals. Over the coming weeks, wolves from around the country came out to support Mr. Wolf and confronted some of the protesting pigs in front of the law offices. Each side waved hateful slogans such as "**Lying Pigs**" and "**Murderous Wolves**." Another bold slogan with the picture of a pig lying face down on a platter read, "**The swine is unclean unto you. Leviticus11:7. You have been warned!**" There was even a picture of a wolf with a noose around his neck, and another grotesque picture of a wolf eating a pig.

CHAPTER EIGHT

PUBLIC OUTCRY

The media frenzy seemed to hit fever-pitch proportions from all angles. The media hogged the story since almost every channel seemed fixated on *Mr. Wolf v. The Three Pigs* in the weeks preceding what appeared to be the civil trial of the century. CNN's Wolf Blitzer announced he would interview Mr. Wolf and his wife.

It was blustering cold out, so many of the pigs bundled up in their winter garb as they yelled at the top of their lungs.

"We will occupy the areas surrounding CNN until Mr. Wolf's invitation is rescinded." Dozens of police officers dressed in riot gear pepper sprayed overzealous protesters who yelled, "It is our First Amendment right to assemble and protest this interview with the devil."

Some yelled chants like, "Hey, hey, ho, ho, CNN has got to go, if they let Mr. Wolf on their show."

Despite the pigs' protest, CNN issued a statement that the interview would go on as planned. The pigs were livid as many of the wolves cheered from their tree-covered domicile and local sports clubs as they raised their glasses in salute to the brave Wolf Blitzer.

On the day of the scheduled television interview, Mr. Wolf's stomach rumbled and twisted into pretzel-like knots as he contemplated what he would say in his first public appearance since the lawsuit made headlines. As he sat at CNN in a maize-colored dressing room scantily furnished with just a table and vanity, the makeup artist dusted Mr. Wolf's face with powder to defuse the shine threatening to form on his fur. This would be Mr. Wolf's first televised interview, and he needed it to go well. Mrs. Wolf, an unwilling participant, was seated a few doors away, quite miserable as her face was pruned into submission with various shades of color by several attendants, while others poked and prodded her thinning hair as they tried to tame it into compliance with glops of gel. Mrs. Wolf felt like quite a specimen. The stylist pushed and pulled Mrs. Wolf in and out of dresses.

Around the studio, camera operators bustled back and forth, as they readied for the segment of Mr. and Mrs. Wolf. Meanwhile the Associated Press kept the anchors busy as breaking news filtered into CNN. Two hours later, Mr. Wolf and Counsel Boar were ready for their "Up close and personal" with the cameras as they emerged from the respective dressing rooms after hours of preening.

Mrs. Wolf, despite her initial misgivings, was rather pleased with the way her hair shimmered under the bright lights in its elegant chignon. *Her hair had never looked so good, and the best part of this*, she thought, *was she had not spent a penny. Maybe Mr. Wolf filing this lawsuit had not been so bad*, Mrs. Wolf thought as she smiled. She stared in wonderment at the face mirrored before her, not quite believing the beauty staring back at her. "You still look good for an old broad," Mrs. Wolf said to her reflection in the mirror as she pretended to pat her hair. The stylist, feeling quite relieved after a rather tense session, responded with peals of laughter. Mr. Wolf let out a loud whistle when he saw his wife and he gave her the high paw salute. He was quite pleased with her appearance. Mr. Wolf grabbed Mrs. Wolf by the arm and said, "Let's knock 'em dead" before the trio was ushered into the studio and outfitted with earpieces and microphones. As the blinding glare from the camera hit his face, Mr. Wolf's chest caved into his stomach. He felt suddenly struck with the enormity of what he was facing. Meanwhile, Counsel Boar was in his element as he beamed into the cameras. Mrs. Wolf looked nonplussed as she sat in her finery pretending it was an everyday occurrence for her to be in front of millions of viewers. She hoped she did not look too shiny.

After Mr. Blitzer dressed in a blue blazer and red satin tie, the camera operator signaled that he could begin his nightly segment of *The Situation Room*. He stared directly into the camera as the show's familiar music played in the background and said, "Tonight we have breaking news as we have the long-awaited interview with the plaintiff in the case of *Mr. Wolf v. The Three Pigs*. Mr. Wolf, the plaintiff in the case, his wife, and attorney Counsel Boar are all here tonight and we at CNN welcome them." Wolf Blitzer turned to face Mr. Wolf and asked, "Now, can you tell our viewers why you decided to take The Three Pigs to court after all these years?"

Mr. Wolf looked at Counsel Boar, who shot him an encouraging nod, before speaking.

"I want to clear my name and the names of all wolves, and I am even pondering a class action suit on behalf of all wolves harmed by the despicable lies of The Three Pigs," Mr. Wolf said. The interview lasted about twenty minutes and then Mr. Wolf was free to go.

Some pigs thought the interview with Wolf Blitzer was biased. Pigs from all over the world were furious. Pigs from as far as farms in Idaho, upstate New York to England, and Germany wrote CNN calling for the suspension or firing of Wolf Blitzer. Pigs bombarded Fox News with its share of angry e-mails when it decided to interview Mr. Wolf in the days leading up to the trial. Some thought Fox News was not reporting the pre-trial events in a fair and balanced way, but Fox News said they were reporting the news objectively. Some militant pigs argued, "Fox News is just too foxy, and we will never watch anything related to them ever again."

The Coalition of Pigs for Justice was quoted in the media as saying, "What do you expect any way, they are all dogs."

MSNBC reporter Rachael Meadow interviewed the pigs for a refresher of their version of the story. The wolves complained about her interview with the pigs, claiming the whole interview was hogwash and the story had some left leanings to it. BBC News made sure it featured breaking news from *Mr. Wolf v. The Three Pigs*. The Brits were even more fascinated with the case because the story of *The Three Little Pigs* was a beloved family tale that everyone enjoyed. More importantly, one of their own, the talented Ms. Priggly, was one of the attorneys on the case. She had graduated at the top of her class from the oldest university in the country. Furthermore, her great-grandfather, Darfulus Priggly, had started the firm in the mother country.

The creator of *Law and Order*, Dick Wolf, even had a ripped-from-the-headline episode. The episode showed The Three Pigs handcuffed for lying under oath. Hundreds of irate pigs sent in letters of complaints to stations that showed this particular episode, claiming that once again the wolves were able to control the media and smear the pigs. Many of the pigs thought they might get to even the score by getting on the *Oprah Winfrey Network*. However, Oprah told them she would wait and see how the trial turned out, and then she would invite the winner on her network. The pigs were furious.

CHAPTER NINE

THE THREE PIGS STRIKE BACK

The pigs filed their answer to Mr. Wolf's complaint within the required period of forty days, responding to each allegation Mr. Wolf made in his complaint. The Three Pigs denied everything Mr. Wolf alleged in his complaint. One Monday afternoon after lunch, Mr. Wolf opened his front door to a loud knock. Big Willy, the process server, stood menacingly in the doorway on crossed hind legs and shoved the court papers at Mr. Wolf.

"You are hereby summoned to appear before the magistrate, the most honorable Judge, to answer for your crimes, Mr. Wolf," Big Willy oinked in a deep voice. Big Willy known to make fancy speeches when he delivered court papers, seemed especially pleased as he doubled over with laughter.

"You are quite welcome," replied Mr. Wolf calmly, "but remember, he who laughs last laughs best."

"That's why you have been served," said Big Willy, tipping his big black hat mockingly as he trotted away proudly down the narrow grassy path. When the story hit the airwaves on the evening news, the pigs were ecstatic. "Now, the truth about this shameless wolf will be the defining shot heard around the world," commented Brick House Pig before switching off the television.

COURT OF MAPLEWOOD
CIVIL COURT

---x

MR. WOLF

                                Plaintiff,   Index Number: 12345

    Vs.

BRICK HOUSE PIG
STRAW HOUSE PIG   **VERIFIED ANSWER**
STICK HOUSE PIG

                         Defendants

---x

The defendants, The Three Pigs, by their respective attorneys, Priggly, Priggly, and Priggly and Pro Se, answering the Verified Complaint of the plaintiff, upon information and belief, respectfully allege:

ANSWERING THE ALLEGED FIRST CAUSE OF ACTION ON BEHALF OF THE PLAINTIFF

Upon information and belief, defendants deny each and every allegation in the paragraphs of the complaint designated as follows:

1.   The Three Pigs are without knowledge or information sufficient to form a belief as to the truth of the allegations contained in paragraph 1 of the complaint.

2.   The Three Pigs are without knowledge or information sufficient to form a belief as to the truth of the allegations contained in paragraph 2 of the Complaint.

3.   Deny

4.   Deny

5.   Deny

6.   Deny

7.   Deny

8.   Deny

9.   Deny

10.   Deny

11.   Deny

WHEREFORE, the defendants demand judgment against the plaintiff dismissing the complaint herein as against the defendant, together with the costs and disbursements of this action and for such other and further relief as to this court may seem just and proper.

Dated: April 20th of This Year

Yours, etc.

Priggly, Priggly, and Priggly
Law Offices of Priggly, Priggly and Priggly,
Attorney for Defendants
555-523-5656

Cc:

Counsel Boar, Attorney for Mr. Wolf

Brick House Pig, Straw House Pig, Stick House Pig, being first duly sworn affirm that they have read the foregoing complaint and that they know the content thereof, and that the same is true, except those matters therein stated to be upon information and belief, and as to those matters, they believe to be true.

The Three Pigs, Defendants
Sworn and subscribed before me May 24th of This Year
Notary Public, John Brown, Maplewood
My commission expires Dec 16, of This Year

CHAPTER TEN

TIME TO SEE THE JUDGE

Ms. Priggly, who was representing two of the pigs, filed a motion on behalf of Brick House Pig and Stick House Pig to dismiss the case. Ms. Priggly argued statute of limitations.

"Your Honor, the actions that this Complaint references happened many years ago. I believe the statute of limitations has passed." Ms. Priggly looked at the Judge and smiled her sweetest smile. The Judge, a female whom Ms. Priggly had never had the misfortune to encounter in court before, stared at Ms. Priggly unflinchingly as her sable colored eyes drilled holes in Ms. Priggly.

"In addition, Mr. Wolf should have raised that issue eons ago," Ms. Priggly said.

The Judge by then seemed worn out by the legal wrangling between the attorneys, sharply replied, "Ms. Priggly, your motion is denied. You should have raised the statute of limitations in the answer you previously filed with the court. It is too late to make that motion now."

Ms. Priggly fumed as she thought about her careless law assistant, Alice, who had filed the wrong answer minus the Affirmative defense of the expiration of the statute of limitations. *I am glad that I fired that lazy pig for making a costly mistake that propelled the case to trial. Next time I will hire employees strictly based on qualifications rather than political favors. Nepotism is not a good thing: now I cannot get this case dismissed as I had hoped,* she thought. Although Ms. Priggly was fuming inwardly, she smiled at the Judge, hoping to work her charm on her.

Several weeks later, Judge Hognott was the Judge assigned to the motion part of the court. It was rumored he might be the presiding judge in the trial of *Mr. Wolf v. The Three Pigs.* Many thought Judge Hognott to be a mean judge, and could not wait until his retirement in a few months. Those who knew him best said he was an old stick in the mud, and Ms. Priggly hoped that, if he were the judge assigned to the case, by the end of the trial he would see things her way. She was not known as a skilled litigator for nothing. In the weeks leading up to the trial, attorneys for both sides filed numerous motions to suppress evidence and witnesses. Miss Priggly tried to keep damaging evidence about the pigs out and Mr. Wolf's attorney, Counsel Boar, tried to keep certain evidence in. The Judge repeatedly asked both sides if the evidence they wanted admitted was relevant to the case. The hearings seemed to go on forever as each side made passionate pleas to Judge Hognott to grant its motions. It seemed that as one issue was resolved, another attorney would file a motion. To the Judge, it seemed the motions just kept coming.

Ms. Priggly also filed a motion to have separate trials for her two clients. She felt they would have a chance at winning if their trials were separate from Straw House Pig. Counsel Boar filed a motion to suppress evidence about Mr. Wolf's prior run-in with another pig. The Judge almost denied Counsel Boar's motion after Ms. Priggly argued relevancy and probative value because the facts of the case with the pigs were important to deciding this present case with Mr. Wolf. However, when Counsel Boar pointed out how long ago the incident occurred, the Judge decided it was too old to have any probative value. Counsel Boar also put in a motion to change the location or venue of the court case.

"Your Honor," he argued, "this court is located right in the heart of Pig Town. Mr. Wolf will never get a fair trial in this county." Judge

64

Hognott denied that motion, arguing that there were enough fair-minded citizens in Maplewood that Mr. Wolf could get a fair trial.

Finally, Judge Hognott said, "I have had enough of this preamble. Filing motions end here. The case will proceed to trial since it appears the lawyers are not willing to act like adults and settle this silly case." He turned to Straw House Pig, who was present in the courtroom, and said, "Get an attorney! Only a fool would represent herself, especially in a case such as this."

"I am too poor to get a lawyer, and the Constitution allows me the right to an attorney based on the Sixth Amendment," Straw House Pig replied. Straw House Pig felt proud of herself for the first time for speaking so intelligently. One of her friends had informed her of this, and she wanted to impress the Judge.

Judge Hognott glared at her as if she was an imbecile. In a sarcastic voice, he replied, "If you had read the Sixth Amendment of the Constitution carefully and intelligently, you would note that those accused of a crime do indeed have the right to an attorney. However, since this is a civil case and not a criminal case, the right to an attorney does not apply, Ms. Smarty Pants." The smile on Straw House Pig's face disappeared as the reality of Judge Hognott's words dawned on her.

"Well, then, Ms. Straw House Pig, the ball is in your court," Judge Hognott admonished as his arctic glare sent chills through her 300-pound frame. "I advise you to get an attorney, and quick."

Straw House Pig's face turned ashen with fright as she considered her predicament. She absolutely could not afford an attorney. Dismissing Straw House Pig, Judge Hognott promptly moved on to setting a court date less than a month away for the start of the trial.

"However," Judge Hognott said as he surveyed the lawyers and their clients, "I hope good faith and common sense will prevail and this case will be settled before then. Trials waste the court's time, tie up the courtrooms, and cost the taxpayers thousands of dollars." That said; Judge Hognott stormed out of the courtroom, his heavy, black, judicial robe and thick, long, silver hair flying behind him.

CHAPTER ELEVEN

SETTLE THIS CASE

By the time the settlement hearing rolled around, it was quite clear neither side was close to reaching an agreement. Ms. Priggly, with her gang of associates and her two clients Brick House Pig and Stick House pig, stared Counsel Boar down as they sat across the long wide table that seem to reflect the divide between the two sides. They collectively used their eyes to shoot darts and arrows at Counsel Boar whenever the Judge assigned to the conference, a tall gangly pig named Judge Arnold, was preoccupied with his law clerks. Noticeably absent was Straw House Pig. Judge Arnold was dressed in a plain blue suit and seemed quite bored as he announced the proceedings for the conference.

Ms. Priggly, dressed in a red cranberry two-piece pantsuit, appeared ready to do battle as her makeup danced like war paint before Counsel Boar's eyes. Counsel Boar stared at Ms. Priggly and her team unblinkingly. His head was alive with busy thoughts as he watched this scene unfold before him. He was not going to let this pint-sized attorney and her minions intimidate him. *This pig is half my size*, he thought, watching his adversaries through half-closed eyes as if he were sleeping.

Mr. Wolf, on the other hand, nervously watched the female lawyer and her associates as they tried to size him up. Brick House Pig and Stick House Pig avoided looking at Mr. Wolf. Instead, they busied themselves with pretend conversations.

Ms. Priggly smiled; she was about to put an end to this farce of a meeting. The trial was her exit plan, and it was then she would gobble up the wolf and his bloated attorney. Ms. Priggly smiled wickedly. Counsel Boar did not return the smile, seeing the loops turning in Ms. Priggly's pretty head. The temperature in the room shot up rapidly as the parties flexed their legal muscles. Counsel Boar named a sum while Ms. Priggly nearly cackled. She muted her expression before she fixed her gaze on her opponents and said, "I must confer with my clients." The two pigs and Ms. Priggly left the room, returning shortly. Their lips formed a collective no as they stared at Mr. Wolf and Counsel Boar.

The Judge sighed; it was going to be a long day. Both parties pretended they wanted to arrive at an agreement when everyone knew it was not going to happen today or ever. The lawyers had written the ending and settlement was not in the script. Counsel Boar sat on the other side of the long mahogany table in the small, faded, windowless room, quite certain no settlement would occur; but what the Judge wanted, he got, so both parties had to go through the motions in this case of legal chess. Hours later, as the day turned to night, the parties hurled insults at each other. The Judge was beside himself, hoping this conference would die a quick death. His head was pounding like an African drum while he listened to the two parties face off.

As the hours moved in a snail-like crawl, sweat poured down Counsel Boar's face while Ms. Priggly appeared as dry as powder. The parties hardly left the room except to consult with their respective clients. Ten marathon-like hours later, as the Judge was about to stop the proceedings, Straw House Pig skipped into the now packed and sweat-drenched room as impatience hung in the air. Straw House Pig looked like a mass of confusion, decked out in a shiny pink suit and metallic pumps. A dozen pairs of eyes turned to gaze at her.

"And who might you be?" the Judge asked, his eyes popping out of his head as he gazed at Straw House Pig angrily.

"I am one of the defendants in this case," Straw House pig mumbled, trying to reflect cheerfulness she did not feel. She had forgotten about the settlement conference until she had accidently stepped on the yellow postcard in between her tangled clothes as she tried to locate her missing phone. That had been less than an hour ago, and she had hurriedly thrown on the only clean clothes she had left hanging in her closet—hence the pink dress. Both her sisters gazed at her resentfully. Straw House Pig's lateness once again confirmed to them her lack of organization and lackadaisical attitude. Brick House Pig and Stick House Pig stared at each other, transmitting a silent message to each other before returning frostbite stares at their sister.

"You have got to be kidding me," the Judge said as he fixed her with an incredulous stare. "It seems you think you are above the rules, since the timing of this conference was 9:00 a.m. sharp."

He looked at his watch and then at the late pig. As Straw House Pig tried to sputter out a response, the Judge raised his hoof to silence her and said, "This settlement conference is over, and I am mighty glad I am not the Judge who will be dealing with this trial."

The Judge gave all the parties a scathing look and waltzed out of the room, glad to be away from the highly intense drama. His law clerks followed close behind with their cart filled with files, giving the parties a sympathetic look before ducking through the door.

As soon as the clerks left, Ms. Priggly looked at Counsel Boar and said, "It will be a cold day in hell before I settle this case. I'll see you boys in court." She smirked as she and her party exited the conference room. Straw House Pig hurried out behind them even as they ignored her.

Counsel Boar looked at Mr. Wolf with a grimace before saying, "It went just like I thought. Let's go get a bite to eat."

Mr. Wolf nodded and followed Counsel Boar out of the room, hoping the ringing in his ears caused by the shouting he had endured over the past couple of hours would stop. It had definitely been a tiring day, and he knew Mrs. Wolf would not be the least bit sympathetic.

CHAPTER TWELVE

MR. WOLF GOES TO COURT

Mr. Wolf's first foray into the courthouse left an indelible impression on him. He realized for the first time the seriousness of his task. He felt intimidated because he never had the need or desire to go into a courthouse before, and he was quite amazed at its enormous size. There were fourteen floors and over a hundred courtrooms to accommodate the many citizens in the town of Maplewood. Mr. Wolf wondered fleetingly about the many reasons so many people occupied the court.

The decor of the courthouse was quite impressive. Numerous antique gold-framed pictures of pig judges from the past lined the sparkling white painted walls. They were dressed in curly white wigs and shiny black or red robes, but the more recent judges dressed in black shiny robes minus the wigs. Among this slew of pictures mounted along the halls of justice was the solitary picture of a lone wolf looking oddly out of place. Mr. Wolf lingered momentarily to admire the pictures, but he secretly hoped this visual imagery would not be indicative of his experience as he navigated the legal maze. He glanced at the expensive sparkling chandeliers that were swinging ever so slightly from the high panel dark wood ceilings. The rhythmic clip-clop of swiftly moving feet along the shiny black marble floor almost sounded musical as court patrons moved back and forth in rapid succession. A group of lawyers recognizable by their clone-like crisp blue Armani suits, expensive Coach and Gucci leather briefcases, and the brown folders they carried dominated the section of the courthouse labeled "Wills, Trusts, and Estates." Other lawyers were engaged in conversations with their clients, who were dressed in various states of attire from Donna Karan and many other high-end designers.

One expensively dressed client asked a lawyer with an expressionless face, "When will this estate settle?"

Another client, who was wearing an off-the-rack dress, appeared somewhat confused by the whole process and yelled, "I need this money soon; she's been dead over a year."

One lawyer tried to calm her client, who appeared quite impatient and disgruntled. In a soothing voice she said, "I will talk to the Judge."

Other attorneys who looked quite peeved yelled into their iPhones and Blackberries as they fired out directives concerning motions and legal briefs to their assistants.

In a packed section labeled Tenants and Landlord, lawyers were yelling at other lawyers, who in turn yelled at clients, "Why didn't you pay your rent?"

Mr. Wolf hurriedly left this part of the courthouse in quest of the civil section for lawsuits. As he rounded a corner, he noticed a label that read "Criminal Proceedings." In this section, the former white corridor seemed to transform into a dreary grey area that boiled over with the raw emotions of clientele discontent. The highly charged atmosphere of discontent seemed to wrestle with the stifled feelings of fear, anger, and resignation evident in the eyes of the wild-eyed defendants.

Mr. Wolf noted that those caught up in this tangled maze of hopelessness were countless wolves and a few pigs. The starring roles in this criminal drama were the defendants of a certain class cast in opposing roles against the state of Maplewood. It appeared the costume of choice for the defendants of Maplewood was loose-fitting baggy jeans with grungy T-shirts. Two wolves, one with a black and white prison-style jumpsuit and one in a wrinkled business suit sat handcuffed with silver bangles at opposite ends of a hard wood bench with two Maplewood undercover cops closely attached. It seemed the officers and the accused had merged into one. Only the shiny badges that gleamed around their necks distinguished the accused from the power brokers.

The criminal part of the courthouse was rather gloomy and the atmosphere quite intense. The participants in this unfolding theatre were liable to receive a death sentence or to lose their liberty at the discretion of the state. Mr. Wolf thought the stench encircling this ante-chamber provided evidence that many of the defendants had not bathed in days. The lawyers, who identified themselves as Maplewood's legal aid attorneys, wore inexpensive suits. Their clothing illustrated the sharp contrast of the pay grade of attorneys employed by the state, versus attorneys on private retainers. Some of the state legal aid attorneys paraded in jeans and galoshes, making it almost impossible to distinguish between the lawyers and the defendants. However, the many folders they carried, and the briefcase-like suitcases, which they carried on their many jaunts to and from the courthouse, set them apart as they yelled out names of clients they had never met, but now employed to represent.

One lawyer from a private firm dressed in a grey Hugo Boss suit yelled at his client, "Why didn't you tell me the truth? You made me look like a fool in front of the Judge." The client, a rather tall wolf with purple-streaked hair and a heavily tattooed arm tried to defend himself.

"I didn't think anyone would find out," he said, but the smartly dressed pig attorney quickly cut him off.

"You will get my bill in the mail, you imbecile. I hope you rot in prison." The attorney appeared quite irate as he strode away looking like he could spit fire. His stomping feet echoed through the hallway as he strode toward the elevator. Mr. Wolf gulped nervously as he heard this exchange.

A few lawyers huddled in a dark corner sipping Cinnamon Dolce Latte from Starbucks. They were complaining about the long hours, low wages, and too many clients. One solitary wolf attorney seated on a hard brown bench was overheard telling a client in an exasperated voice, "You are the fifteenth defendant I have had today; how do you plead?" The defendant, a pig dressed in tight-fitting slacks and an overly rumpled blouse looked to be on the verge of tears. Mr. Wolf felt despondent as he watched this scene unfold, so he made a swift retreat to meet Counsel Boar, afraid to be captured in this web of confusion. This floor of the court building was definitely not for the likes of him, Mr. Wolf thought.

Remembering that he had to meet Counsel Boar on the twelfth floor in room 1208, part B., Mr. Wolf strode purposefully toward the black elevator. The elevator measured a mere four and a half feet by six feet, but it was jam-packed with countless passengers refusing to budge even as the double doors refused to close. Several court officers forcefully extracted passengers as their collective weight had exceeded the 2,500-pound capacity of the elevator. Those wedged tightly together in the back of the elevator gasped for air and yelled loudly, "GET OUT, YOU CAN'T FIT."

Many quite harried as they tried to make it to their morning appointments. Mr. Wolf finally decided to take the stairwell to the right of the elevator, not wanting to enter into the combustion he had just witnessed.

As he strode into the courtroom, the first sight that assailed him was the scales of justice etched in black on the cream-colored wall directly above the Judge's bench. He spied Counsel Boar engaged in a heated conversation with another pig attorney who was laughing hysterically at something Counsel Boar said. Counsel Boar motioned for him to take a seat before the proceedings got underway. The short stocky attorney Counsel Boar was speaking with peeked over at Mr. Wolf and sneered disdainfully. Mr. Wolf gulped nervously, hoping he was doing the right thing by having this pig represent him. Mr. Wolf took a seat on one of the hard benches facing the Judge's chambers as he waited for the court proceedings to begin. The courtroom began to fill up as the court officer yelled that the court proceedings were about to commence.

CHAPTER THIRTEEN

SHOW ME YOUR EVIDENCE

Several weeks later, the discovery process commenced. During the discovery phase of the case, both attorneys hounded the opposing sides with requests for all types of documents.

Counsel Boar asked opposing counsel to produce the building permit for the straw house and stick house. Ms. Priggly asked Counsel Boar to produce documentation of Mr. Wolf's so-called injuries. Also during the discovery phase, Mr. Wolf was deposed and so were The Three Pigs. The deposition process was similar to a trial, as each side had to submit to questioning from opposing counsel. The process took place away from the courthouse and the lawyers for the plaintiff and defendant used the opposing sides answer to discredit them at trial.

The door to the Judge's chamber opened, and Judge Hognott walked up to the podium.

"That is Judge Hognott," Ms. Priggly whispered to one of her associates.

"I heard about him," the associate replied. "He is the grumpy old pig who wears that badly fitting old grey wig. He has a great tan though, because he is always in that tanning salon trying to look good for the females."

Ms. Priggly smiled briefly before replying, "He is a no-nonsense judge, and many attorneys quiver when they hear he is assigned to their case. His reputation of throwing both clients and attorneys in jail for contempt of court is well known. Lawyers know they have to be well versed in the rule of law if they want to survive a round in Judge Hognott's courtroom. I do not fear him because he knows that I always do a fabulous job."

"I'm Judge Hognott, and I am presiding over this trial," Judge Hognott announced sternly. "All lawyers involved in this case must submit a list with a complete disclosure of all witnesses to testify at trial because surprises by either side will not be welcomed. This is not TV where we have surprises jumping out of every corner. Neither is this a jack-in-the-box courtroom. I want to run a smooth and orderly court." The Judge looked sternly at the lawyers. "Anyone who disregards my rules will be held in contempt of court." He pounded his hammer-like gavel before abruptly leaving the Judge's podium. He paused when he was about to head into the Judge's chambers and said in a deceptively soft voice, "I will not be made a fool of since I have a reputation to uphold."

With that, the Judge exited the courtroom and slammed his chamber door shut.

"What's eating him?' asked one of the court occupants. "He is oh so dramatic for no reason whatsoever."

CHAPTER FOURTEEN

VOIR DIRE

Two months later, while jury selection was underway, a flock of birds encircled the courthouse. "What's the drama in the courthouse?" Blackbird Bill squawked.

"Word has it that the wolves and the pigs have finally taken their grievances to court," chirped a young jackdaw.

"Seems like Maplewood was abuzz with activity while we were gone south for the winter," replied a Canadian goose.

"Just imagine the wolves, the foxes, the pigs, and the dogs dressed like clowns for the trial," said an old one-eyed pigeon.

"Yea! Yea!" said a parrot. "They are just human wannabes in their frivolous getups."

The whole flock of birds laughed so loudly that the chattering and squawking caught the attention of the crowd below. They looked up in amazement at their feathered friends circling above and wondered at their lightheartedness. On this rather warm morning, the courthouse was swarming with reporters and photographers. The Maplewood police acted as a barricade between the crowd and the court personnel to pre-serve sanity amidst all the melodrama.

"A picture of these merry birds over the courthouse will put a dif-ferent spin on this historic story," said a reporter as he snapped some pictures.

The attorneys who had starring roles in the case of *Mr. Wolf v. The Three Pigs* were in huge demand, especially the high-powered attorney Ms. Priggly, representing Brick House Pig and Stick House Pig. She was reputed to be an aggressive litigator who had never lost a case. Before Ms. Priggly made her way to the dozens of concrete white steps leading to the courthouse, she daintily smoothed her black Peter Pan-collared Versace dress and straightened her cream three-strand Majorica Baroque Pearl necklace nestled around her neck. She care-fully examined her teeth and pink lipstick in her hand mirror as she prepared for her close-up with the media. Her hired bodyguard was on hand to shield her from the chaos.

As the reporters spied Ms. Priggly, they converged upon her, shov-ing microphones and cameras into her path as they pounded her with questions.

"How long do you think the jury selection process will take?"

"What kind of jury are you looking for?"

Ms. Priggly smiled sweetly as she shooed the reporters away before beginning her assent to the courthouse. She assumed an erect posture and picked up her gait to distance herself from the press. The black Manolo Blahnik studded snake-heeled pumps fitted snuggly on her hooves and squeaked noisily as she mounted the steps. She skillfully maneuvered the Cognac Double Gusset Top Zip Milano briefcase that bobbed up and down at her side. Ms. Priggly was quite satisfied with the press coverage the case had received thus far.

The jury selection process for the trial of *Mr. Wolf v. The Three Pigs* was chaotic to say the least. The court clerk, Miggy Piggy, told report-ers at Fox Five News, "I have never seen anything like this in all my four decades working at the courthouse. There are literally thousands of volunteers eager to sign up for jury duty. Usually, very few want to serve on the jury except the retired, bored housewives, and those wanting a respite from the monotony of their jobs. I guess the forty dollars a day pittance the state doles out to jurors makes a difference."

"I usually shirk jury duty because it's such a pain," said a fox, "but this is an opportunity that I will not miss."

"Yes! I have always made excuses such as 'I have to work, I don't have time, I have a family, I have no babysitter, I have a business to run,'" replied a wolf, "but by hook or by crook, I want a seat on this jury. Those pigs are not getting away with their lies."

"I usually throw the jury papers in the garbage or just ignore them despite the warning of a thousand-dollar fine or a warrant for my arrest," replied a pig sarcastically. "But this evil wolf will have me to contend with if he thinks that we pigs are going to let him get away with this, he is wrong." He looked at the wolves around the courthouse disdainfully.

The sensationalism surrounding the upcoming trial of *Mr. Wolf v. The Three Pigs* attracted dogs, rabbits, wolves—you name it. They lined up around the courthouse, in the halls of the courthouse, and in the clerk's office pleading to be jurors. Therefore, Ms. Miggy Piggy told the reporters at *Fox 5 News*, "Please inform the public that jury duty is not voluntary. The court must officially summons a potential juror. It is required that one must be born in Maplewood, or be a naturalized citizen. In addition, you cannot be a convicted felon and must be over eighteen years of age." Though these requirements headlined the news, the would-be jurors disregarded Clerk Miggy Piggy and continued to pack the vicinity surrounding the courthouse.

"I refuse to listen to that old biddy; I can beat the odds and be selected as a juror, so I can sell my story to the tabloids for millions of dollars. This is my ticket to success," said Porky Pig, the Postmaster.

In the days leading up to the trial, anyone who received papers for court felt they had won the lottery even though some found out the hard way that many are called, but few are chosen. Only twelve jurors and two alternates would be lucky enough to gain this coveted prize. Some prospective jurors were even reading up on the odds of being selected for jury duty. Many scoured the internet feverishly searching for the profiles of past high profile jurors. Amidst the excitement, reporters tried to pack the courtroom during the *voir dire* process as the attorneys for Mr. Wolf and The Three Pigs questioned the potential jurors.

The *voir dire* process started when the Judge declared that the parties were about to select a jury in the defamation case of *Mr. Wolf v. The Three Pigs*. Judge Hognott in a time-honored tradition admonished the jurors as follows:

"We estimate this trial will take several weeks or months, and you must respond to the following questions truthfully. Do any of you know anything about this case through personal knowledge, any discussions, the news media, or any other source? Do you know any of the parties such as Mr. Wolf or The Three Pigs? Do you know any of the lawyers, specifically Counsel Boar, Ms. Priggly, or Ms. Sow? Do you have any bias against the plaintiff, Mr. Wolf, or the defendants, The Three Pigs? Is there any reason you cannot give this case your undivided attention and render a fair and impartial verdict? If you answer yes to any of these questions, then you cannot serve."

Many of the potential jurors listening to the Judge knew they could not admit to having any biases since this would disqualify them from serving as jurors.

"If this judge thinks I am going to admit to anything that will disqualify me, he must be crazy," snickered one pig softly as his friends nearby smiled and nodded in agreement.

Who had not heard about this case? Many of the jurors thought to themselves as they stared straight ahead.

One would actually have to be living under a rock to be unaware of the facts in the case of Mr. Wolf v. The Three Pigs, considering the media's minute-by-minute updates through the twenty-four-hour news cycle, they thought. Additionally, the case dubbed the trial of the century filled the conversations of the many citizens of Maplewood.

As the Judge prattled on with his instructions, a brown-faced dog closed his eyes with a half smile on his face and thought, *I am going to*

*become a celebrity making appearances on televisions all over the world
and making millions off this famous case.*

"I NEED YOUR UNDIVIDED ATTENTION," shouted the Judge,
looking at the dog sternly. Feeling embarrassed, the dog looked around
the courtroom to see if anyone witnessed his humiliation and then
looked at the Judge intently.

Ms. Priggly watched the dozens of potential jurors as they waited,
hoping the lawyers would select them.

*I am not worried about picking the right jury for this trial because
my hired experts will select jurors that are most likely to vote in favor of
the pigs,* she thought to herself. The firm in question was Jurorexpert
Inc., which had a reputation for selecting the right jurors for cases. Ms.
Priggly had used them several times before and thus far, she had never
lost a case.

Some argued that justice was blind, but jurors were not, and Ms.
Priggly knew she needed jurors biased in favor of the pigs. She smiled
with satisfaction since she knew that would not be too hard to do. She
was eavesdropping on a conversation between two of her experts, and
she felt satisfied with the trend of the conversation.

"Wolves have a bad reputation," the experts whispered, "and we
just have to exploit the bad sentiments to our advantage and carefully
choose the right jurors."

Counsel Boar stood in front of the courtroom, and looked at the
long parade of potential jurors. He also studied Ms. Priggly now surrounded by her fleet of jury consultants. The consultants outfitted with
white lab coats and identical laptop computers eagerly cranked out a
host of probabilities based on the vital statistics and the demograph-
ics of potential jurors in the jurisdiction of Maplewood. The Jurorexpert Inc. advisors looked more suited for a sterile science lab than a
noisy claustrophobic courtroom. Ms. Priggly listened intently as they
scrolled out their analysis on a carpet-length chart of jurors who they
felt would decide in favor of the pigs. One of the analysts droned on
in a nasal voice about the infinite possibilities. Some of the stats as
configured read:

Jurors likely to hit a home run for the pigs:

Species	Pig
Level of Education	less than high school
Profession	None; look for bored housewives, persons doing menial jobs
Gender	Female
Age	Older than the MTV crowd

Potential Prejudices:

People who hated wolves, and believed the pigs were the victims in the story of The Three Little Pigs.

One analyst read off a long list of characters that the jury pool should avoid:

"Liberals, freethinkers, flower-pigs, anyone who suffers from any type of affliction, anyone who feels he or she is a victim of oppression, teachers, professors, lawyers, therapists, social workers, people not born in Maplewood, East Coast and West Coast Pigs, or anyone with wolf friends, married to a wolf, related to a wolf, neighbors with a wolf, or went to schools with a wolf."

Ms. Priggly scanned the jurors, looking for converts to her cause. Her brain sizzled with endless possibilities as she perused the courtroom for potential jurors who would perform like puppets on a string for the court. She watched her opponent, Counsel Boar, suspiciously. He was dressed in an all-white suit that reminded her of a stuffed egg that was about to crack.

Counsel Boar was quite certain Ms. Priggly would argue that wolves had dangerous propensities. As he watched Ms. Priggly contemplatively, he believed he could literally see the wheels in her brain spinning furiously as she sized up the jurors. *Ms. Priggly is a worthy adversary based on her reputation as a highly skilled trial attorney and her performance thus far*, he thought. *Furthermore, it is a known fact that Ms. Priggly has never lost a case, though I hope that is about to change.*

Despite the Judge's warning, speculation filled the blogosphere as to who would win the trial of the century. One blog in particular called www.thethreepiggyliars.com claimed that the wolves would win because the truth was on their sides. The site crashed after the first day when millions of users from around the world in places such as Africa, North America, South America, Central America, Asia, Europe, Australia, The Middle East, Antarctica, Ukraine, and the Caribbean posted comments in over fifty languages defending a wide spectrum of positions. Some claimed the pigs were responsible for crashing the site because they did not want the truth told. Later that day, the site posted that it was experiencing technical difficulty and was trying to acquire more gigabits.

The pigs launched their own sites called www.bigbadwolf.com and www.dontbelievethewolf.com. In China, their internet version known as, Weibo experienced difficulties as people debated the issues of *Mr. Wolf v. The Three Pigs*. Pigs and wolves in Alaska huddled in their igloos as they posted their comments about Mr. Wolf on Facebook. In response, some wolves took out ads in the *Times* encouraging wolves to come out and defend their good name. The next day the pigs placed an ad in the *Times* on the adjacent page that read, "**Wolf desperation is at a fever pitch in the trial of the century. Don't be blindsided by the desperate underhanded tactics of the adversary.**" One particular pig quoted on page six of the *Post,* said "This is a slam dunk case for the pigs: be assured that we will put the wolves to shame."

A pack of wolves had converged at the Hot Spot hamburger joint to discuss the case. Biggie Wolf read the pigs' advertisement in the *Times* to the group, and they bared their teeth in dismay and howled angrily.

"What insolent arrogance! Do they know something we don't know?" asked Grandpa Gruff, a retired schoolteacher.

Mr. Wolf wondered who was helping these moronic pigs. They seem to be getting rather intelligent by the day.

As the spectators fought via the internet and the media for support in the court of public opinion, the real court case moved along as the opposing counsels battled using legal texts and precedents.

CHAPTER FIFTEEN

WHAT IS A PIG TO DO TO GET AN ATTORNEY?

Later, Straw House Pig lay undressed on her damp, stained, brownish-grey mattress in her smelly apartment recounting the day's happenings. She felt paralyzed with fear, considering her predicament. She was without a lawyer in a complex game of chess, about to be checkmated by Mr. Wolf. Straw House Pig did not know where she was going to get money to pay a lawyer. After the preliminary proceedings at the courthouse, she timidly approached her sisters and pleaded with them once again, "Please lend me some money; I am poor and broke, and you are the only family I have."

Both sisters looked at her almost pitifully as they glided out of court. Their faces as usual reflected no sympathy toward her, just the usual stony disdain she had grown accustomed to since childhood.

"We have no money to lend, just barely enough to take care of our own expenses," they chorused as they pushed past her.

Could they have rehearsed that line? Straw House Pig wondered. She noted a badly disguised reporter frantically taking notes as the flashing light of a camera went off, but she had been too troubled to care.

At home, after resting for a while, Straw House Pig donned a fluffy pink bathrobe. Her mind was too preoccupied with her troubles to notice the smell of the leftover stale food and rats scrambling for cover when she entered her apartment. She spent hours looking around her disorganized pen for a telephone book. She rummaged through the Maplewood yellow pages, searching frantically in the advertising section for a lawyer. She forcefully punched the numbers on the phone as she spotted the first lawyer's number under the letter *A*. She repeated this process for a good few hours, but the exorbitant prices scared her off until she decided to change her tactic. She sighed, thinking that the alphabet system had never worked for her, so she started plucking lawyers at random from the phone book.

"Hello, Pig and Company Law Firm, how can I help you?" replied the voice at the end of the phone line that Straw House Pig had dialed.

"I am the youngest pig in the case of *Mr. Wolf v. The Three Pigs* and I need a lawyer to take my case."

"Hold on, darling, let me get the lawyer on the line," the receptionist replied excitedly.

"Jetsam speaking," a deep voice said after a few seconds.

"Mr. Jetsam, can you take my case? I need a lawyer badly. Can you help me, please?"

"That's a high-profile case, and my fee is a hundred thousand dollars. Retainer's fee is ten thousand dollars. When can you come in to sign a retainer agreement and make the initial deposit?" asked the lawyer.

"I have no money, but can you bon praw my case?" she asked in a small voice.

"Ha! Ha! Ha! You mean pro bono, my dear. I am sorry; I have a very busy schedule, and I can't work for free."

Straw House Pig tried several other attorneys who had volunteered to take her case pro bono for the publicity, but wanted her to pay money up front just in case she lost. When they realized she was broke, she never heard back from them. Her many calls to their offices went unanswered or unreturned. As it stood, she could barely keep food on her table. She was just a paycheck away from being broke and always seconds away from eviction, as her grumpy old landlord habitually chased her down for his late rent. She had even spent some time on the government dole until the city of Maplewood had sent her a nasty one-page letter stating that she was ineligible for assistance because she was an able-bodied pig without dependents. This had ended Straw House Pig's romp with the government. She was now all alone, moving from place to place like a nomad without a set destination.

Straw House Pig knew her sisters would not be the least sympathetic to her plight since they felt this was all her fault. Furthermore, due to their outright indifference to her many hysterical pleas, she knew she was alone in a legal maze masterminded by the evil Mr. Wolf. Consequently, Straw House Pig went to a Maplewood bookstore to buy some self-help books. Before leaving the apartment, she put on a pair of oversized sunglasses and a haphazardly tied headscarf, hoping to mask her identity. She was tired of the curious stares from onlookers and the taunting from some of the Maplewood wolves. As she searched intently through the shelves of the bookstore, she found books with titles such as *How to Think like a Lawyer* in *Five Days, Lawyering for Dummies*, and *How to Represent Yourself*. She waited patiently in line and prayed to see the words approved when she swiped her credit card. When it was her turn, she watched nervously as the cashier totaled her purchase.

"Your total is fifty-five dollars and seventy-five cents," the bubble-gum-popping cashier finally said as she watched Straw House Pig skeptically. Straw House pig swiped her card and breathed a sigh of relief when the purchase was accepted.

Straw House Pig spent many days sitting on the floor of her apartment reading her self-help books. Cramping pain ripped through her legs as she pored over tons of pages with incomprehensible words. For the zillionth time, she regretted not completing high school or going to college. At least then, she might have been able to understand the books. Straw House Pig even tried drafting her own legal motions, but the clerks rejected the motions for several reasons: failure to follow directions, failure to use proper format, failure to sign document, failure to comply with deadlines, and the list went on. She cried in frustration, now realizing why lawyers charged so much money.

"This legal stuff requires too much time to understand the laws, to write it in that legal language the lawyers speak, and then to follow the stupid rules about deadlines and serving papers," she muttered to herself. She buried her head in her hooves as she contemplated her fate.

"I feel like I am on a sinking ship without a life jacket and I hope I will not be humiliated by an unfair legal system," she cried hysterically.

CHAPTER SIXTEEN

MEDIA FRENZY

Judge Hognott put a gag order on the lawyers to prevent them from discussing the case with the press. Nevertheless, someone leaked information concerning the motions filed by the various attorneys. Judge Hognott was furious when he read some of the comments in the newspapers and listened to the mainstream media.

"He is an old idiotic judge who is not following the rules of evidence," one reporter even joked.

"What law school did he attend?"

"Maybe he bought his degree," one commentator stated his face quite serious.

One radio talk show host even joked that the court stenographer, Betty Sue, seemed more interested in the antics going on in the courtroom than doing her job of recording each day's proceedings. The reporter made this comment due to several instances when Betty Sue was unable to read back courtroom proceedings that occurred only minutes earlier.

The scene outside the courtroom during the weeks leading up to the trial was chaotic, to say the least. Scores of blue and white police barricades were clearly visible as the Maplewood police tried to maintain order, separating Mr. Wolf's supporters from The Three Pigs' supporters. They had commandeered the steps of the courthouse with placards and shouted interchangeably in unison, "DOWN WITH THE PIGS" and "FRY MR. WOLF."

The lines to the courthouse were several blocks deep, and overzealous court officers guarded every entrance. They frisked everyone for weapons, phones, and cameras and watched the line so closely that it appeared as if they were babysitting the swarm of spectators who formed a mass around the courthouse premises. Many fights broke out in the procession of wolves and pigs as they tried to settle their differences on the street.

"THIS IS STREET JUSTICE, AND IT'S ABOUT TIME WE TAKE MATTERS IN OUR OWN HANDS," SHOUTED A PACK OF ANGRY WOLVES.

The pigs squealed back, "Oh no, it's gross unfairness. You are nothing but bullies about to lose your case again."

All other cases on the court's calendar came to a grinding halt, as the trial of *Mr. Wolf v. The Three Pigs* got under way. Litigants sent hundreds of their complaints to the mayor of Maplewood as their cases came to a halt because of the trial of *Mr. Wolf v. The Three Pigs*. Supporters of both parties camped out in tents in close proximity to the courthouse for several months, holding vigils for their respective parties. Some of the spectators had driven in from other states and some flew in from other countries hoping to be a part of the trial of the century. Hotels in close proximity to the courthouse and around the city soon filled. Many were without a vacancy for months. The number of tourists to Maplewood during the trial was unprecedented. Each day visitors from neighboring cities drove many gas miles to Maplewood to join the multitude around the courthouse.

Prior to the start of the first day of trial, dozens of reporters lined up around the court building hoping to get pictures and interviews with

Mr. Wolf, The Three Pigs, and the attorneys. Several media personalities pursued Ms. Priggly aggressively for interviews. Most of them knew her personally and remained fascinated by her notoriety from previous high-profile cases. They simply loved her dramatic flair and sharp legal mind.

Several news helicopters circled the courthouse, signifying the high-profile nature of *Mr. Wolf v. The Three Pigs*. As the parties involved in the case arrived, reporters and journalists excitedly transmitted reports to their respective news outlets. On the ground, scores of reporters held microphones with signature names of national and international news media. They all competed for strategic locations where they would have access to the first bit of news releases.

Shortly before the start of the 9:30 a.m. trial, Ms. Priggly exited a chauffeured-driven red crisp convertible with two of her associates from the world-renowned Law Firm of Priggly, Priggly and Priggly. A stocky and muscle-bound Pit Bull sprinted nimbly from the car and shielded her from the onslaught of reporters who rushed to get her first statement for their own headlines. He was a famous bodyguard with a no-nonsense attitude and was reputed to spend countless hours in the gym pumping iron. The bodyguard, impressively dressed in a black Armani suit, a black tie, black leather gloves, and dark shades provided Ms. Priggly with much-needed protection against intrusive reporters. Reporters from FOX, TMZ, Channel 7, MSNBC, CNN, BBC, and countless others bolted to interview Ms. Priggly.

"Down, boy," Ms. Priggly said to her bodyguard, as he seemed poised to attack the reporters. His growl subsided into a disappointing sigh because he could not keep the annoying reporters in check. Today Ms. Priggly just smiled at the reporters as they shoved several microphones and cameras in her face. They hurled several questions at her, some shouting at the top of their lungs.

"What is going to happen on the first day of trial?"

"What is your legal strategy against the wolf?"

"Why are you not representing all of The Three Pigs?"

"Who is your first witness?"

In response to the reporters, Ms. Priggly in her usual seductive voice smiled sweetly and said, "Come on, ladies and gents of the media, you know Judge Hognott has issued a gag order that I simply cannot ignore," as she glanced at her diamond studded Cartier watch.

"I will see you at the end of the trial," she continued in her pronounced English accent that they adored.

She took off her designer D&G sunglasses that shielded her gaze from the sun's bright summer glare and the flashing lights of the cameras. Ms. Priggly proudly strutted into the court building, savoring the attention with delight. The gun-toting court officers at the entrance doors waved the annoying reporters away and returned to checking attorney identifications, press passes, and tickets. Many of the paparazzi zeroed in on Ms. Priggly's attire and snapped shots in succession before she disappeared into the courthouse. The reporters frantically e-mailed pictures to the tabloids, eager to be the first to release pictures of the famous Ms. Priggly.

Some of the reporters denied entry into the courthouse looked visibly angry. A few of the reporters relegated to camping out in the scorching summer heat became even angrier as sweat poured from their faces. The punishing heat of the hot sun beat mercilessly down on their bodies as they awaited breaking news from the courthouse. Some of the reporters interviewed a few spectators armed with bottles of ice-cold water and gigantic umbrellas that sheltered them from the hot sun. Many of the spectators camped out in front of the building competed to catch a glimpse of the starring characters in the drama that was about to unfold.

Upon Counsel Boar's arrival, scores of reporters thronged him. They propelled microphones in his face, eager to get a comment.

"How do you feel going up against the high-powered Ms. Priggly?" one reporter asked.

"The race is not for the swift, nor the battle for the strong," he replied.

"Do you think you can win this case for Mr. Wolf?" another reporter asked.

"I think I can, but only time will tell," he replied.

Counsel Boar gently pushed a microphone aside and purposefully ascended the steps of the courthouse. He disappeared through the doors with his large shoulder bag stacked with papers while inwardly rehearsing his opening statement. Upon entering the courthouse, Counsel Boar could feel the high tension, but he tried to relax his mind so he could clearly deliberate at the opportune time. He looked around the courthouse for Mr. Wolf, but he did not see him, so he walked over to the defense table and carefully arranged his notes so they could be at hand when he needed them.

Counsel Boar glanced to his left, and there was Ms. Priggly shivering with the anticipation and excitement of the moment. She always loved the first day of trial, especially in high-powered cases like this where all eyes focused on her as she delivered her well-rehearsed legal punches. She could not wait to make mincemeat of that treacherous Counsel Boar. Her red Manolo Blahnik D'orsay pumps made clopping sounds announcing her arrival. Ms. Priggly, flanked by her entourage of court officers, associates, and bodyguard, was ushered into an empty elevator away from the throngs of spectators waiting to find their own empty elevator. Mobs of pigs yelled,

"MS. PRIGGLY, WE LOVE YOU," while the icy stares of the wolves directed her way amused her.

CHAPTER SEVENTEEN

I WANT TO SEE MY MOTHER

In an exclusive beauty salon in a posh neighborhood in Maplewood, a hairstylist named Chris clothed in a black smock added five-hundred-dollar-a-pack extensions to a client's mane. The client, whose name was Kourtney, turned her eyes to the TV screen, as excited chatter broke out. Kourtney was waiting for her mother, Stick House Pig, to appear on screen. A manicurist had just flipped the channel to TMZ capturing the mob scene at the courthouse. Kourtney's two luminous grey eyes were now riveted to the fifty-inch screen TV affixed to the pink wall of the upscale salon. Work in the salon paused as the ten workers and their customers watched reporters from around the globe. The desperate reporters circled the courthouse as they pounced on the actors in the unfolding drama of *Mr. Wolf v. The Three Pigs.*

"Hurry up!" Kourtney yelled to her stylist as she spotted her mother entering the courthouse decked out in a blue two-piece Chanel pantsuit. Stick House Pig's hair, cut into an ultra-chic bob, barely touched her chin, and her ears glittered in the sun. Stick House Pig's eyes, covered by shaded glasses, tried to avoid the numerous cameras' intrusive stares. As

Kourtney watched this scene unfold, she knew she had to make it down to the courthouse ASAP. Here was her chance to increase her recognition beyond Maplewood. By the time the trial was done, she would be more famous than Paris Hilton, Kourtney thought. Kourtney grimaced as she once again yelled, "Hurry up" to the model-looking pig doing her hair.

"I am going as fast as I can," Chris replied as he fixed a fake smile on his face, pissed that this want-to-be celebrity brat was trying to order him around.

While time could not move fast enough for Kourtney, her stylist seemed unconcerned with the passage of time as he weaved and watched the screen simultaneously. Kourtney fumed, promising herself that she would never use Chris again, no matter how good Chris did her hair. She needed to get home and change. Kourtney's thoughts abruptly shifted to what she would wear as she quickly texted her friends to meet her at the courthouse.

CHAPTER EIGHTEEN

MR. WOLF V. THE THREE PIGS, TRIAL DAY

The uniformed Bailiff swore the jurors in before the trial commenced.

"Do you solemnly swear that you will decide the issues in this case fairly and honestly, and give a true verdict based only on the evidence presented in this courtroom?

Do you further swear that you have fully and truthfully answered all questions put to you in this matter?"

One of the selected jurors quickly blurted out "No" to the last question.

The Judge removed her from the jury. An alternate quickly replaced this juror. Some of the jurors thought the removed juror had been silly to answer truthfully. If they had followed suit, perhaps no juror would be left to deliberate the case. The Judge substituted the juror, and the Bailiff resumed his questioning.

"Do you further swear that you have fully and truthfully answered all questions put to you in this matter?" This time all the jurors answered "yes."

After the Bailiff instructed the jurors to take a seat, he solemnly said,

"Members of the jury, you have been sworn or affirmed."

Many from the town and elsewhere attempted to pile into the square-shaped courtroom hoping to get one of the few prized seats on the hard wooden black benches. The court officers had to force the doors to the courtroom shut as throngs of supporters unable to enter pushed against the black iron doors. Finally, the officers bolted the doors. The pigs and wolves yelled at the top of their lungs, furious at the officers for denying them access to the courtroom. Their loud wails penetrated the courtroom as the Judge entered. Judge Hognott was furious. As the presiding judge, he ran a tight ship, and he did not care too much for all the publicity surrounding this trial. When he entered the courtroom in a magnificent black robe, the audience rose to their feet as the Bailiff loudly proclaimed, "All rise!"

The Bailiff, a strapping black pig, was neatly dressed in his blue seamed pants and crisp white uniform with his badge prominently displayed on his shirt. The Bailiff's billy club, pepper spray, and gun revealed his power and authority within the confines of the courthouse and nearby vicinity. He was enjoying his role in this high-powered case, so he could not wait for everyone to see he was responsible for keeping order at the trial of *Mr. Wolf v. The Three Pigs*. He did not have a starring role like the Judge, the attorneys, and the parties in the case; nonetheless, his supporting role was a coveted one all the other Bailiffs had hoped to secure. The Bailiff smiled broadly, clearly reveling in his good fortune. He just hoped the cameras would capture his good side on the evening news. He continued to pose for the cameras even as he went about his duty of keeping order.

"Order in the court," said Judge Hognott since he was quite upset about the lack of order in his courtroom at the start of this historic trial. Judge Hognott knew he had to put a stop to this disorder immediately or no one would respect his authority for the duration of the trial. The Judge ordered the Bailiff and court officers to control the apparent chaos outside the courtroom forthwith. As the noise subsided, the jury comprised of seven pigs, three wolves, and two foxes entered the court. They walked single file to their seats in the jury box. All eyes in the courtroom were fixated on the group of twelve and their alternates. The sight of the jury seemed to set off a new set of chatter, so the Bailiff threatened to remove anyone who was talking. Pigs, dogs, foxes, wolves, and rabbits mostly dressed in their finest attire, from evening gowns to cocktail dresses, church dresses with fancy broad-rimmed hats to three-piece suits, quickly ceased their grumbling, fearing they would miss this spectacle. Many fidgeted in their seats as they waited for the trial to begin. Some of them hoped the cameras would capture their profiles and beam it across the screen for the world to see. Others tried to contort themselves between and behind the many humongous hats, hoping to become invisible. It was imperative they avoid the all-seeing eyes of the cameras because they had skipped work or classes.

Judge Hognott cloaked in his familiar black gown sat atop his throne. He surveyed the scene in its entirety, peering at the occupants sternly. As he honed in on the cameras, he tried to conceal his irritation. If he had his way, he would not allow cameras in the courtroom, but in a technologically charged society, that seemed like a dream. Judge Hognott shrugged off his displeasure and started the court proceedings.

CHAPTER NINETEEN

OPENING STATEMENTS

Counsel Boar was a remarkable sight as he began his opening statements. He was dressed in a tan double-breasted suit, a bright pink spotted bow tie, and a pink handkerchief tucked into the left outer breast pocket of his suit. Gold cufflinks and custom-made size ten shiny pink patent leather shoes complemented his attire. As the plaintiff's lawyer, he had to address the court first, since he had the burden of proving the case. Counsel Boar assumed an air of importance and rocked back and forth, proudly twirling a gold stopwatch as he stood before the jurors to present his well-prepared opening argument.

"It has often been said what a tangled web we weave when we practice to deceive," he began, "and this deception has stifled the truth of the matter as it relates to Mr. Wolf, an upstanding member of society."

These bold words clearly and loudly pronounced by Counsel Boar drew veiled snickers from the pigs. Counsel Boar scanned the audience, and looked at The Three Pigs sitting on the bench, sandwiched between their attorneys, at the front of the courtroom. He walked over to the jurors, who were staring at him with rapt attention.

"Members of the jury," he said as he held on to the partition that enclosed the jurors. "This is a case about defamation, slander, and libel. Please do not let these seemingly big words scare you. These three words are just fancy words for lies, lies, and more lies, as told by the then-Three Little Pigs. It does not matter if they are in written form or orally communicated, they are still lies.

"Here in written form is the libelous evidence," he said, as he brandished a copy of the book written by the pigs. It depicted an unflattering mug shot of Mr. Wolf on its cover for all to see. Loud groans and laughter came from the audience, so the Judge bellowed,

"ORDER IN THE COURT!"

Counsel Boar spun around abruptly and pointed at The Three Pigs in the front row, who stared straight ahead as if they were statues in a wax museum.

"THESE PIGS LIED ON MR. WOLF,"

Counsel Boar bellowed as his thunderous voice rumbled through the courtroom. The Three Pigs cowered in their seats, as Counsel Boar's eyes seemed to pierce them like daggers. "The First Amendment of the Constitution, the highest law in the land, protects free speech; however, these rights are not absolute since the Constitution does not protect lies." Counsel Boar switched his gaze from the pigs to the jurors.

"Defamation is a lie that hurts. Consequently, our Constitution does not protect it." Counsel Boar surveyed the rest of the courtroom while wiping sweat from his brow. Rows of fascinated eyes stared at the lawyer, hungry for the litigious feast in which they were about to partake.

"We will prove in the days ahead that Mr. Wolf was defamed by these three not-so-little pigs sitting in the front row," Counsel Boar continued as he pointed at Straw House Pig, Brick House Pig, and Stick House Pig. Straw House Pig squirmed in her seat, while her sisters sat poker faced.

"The judge will instruct you in the weeks to come that defamation is a false statement communicated to a third party that causes harm to a person's reputation. The evidence will show that The Three Pigs lied on Mr. Wolf, communicated these lies about Mr. Wolf to others, and caused infinite harm to his reputation by sullying it. As a result, Mr. Wolf has been forced to live out his life in virtual exile."

The short end of Counsel Boar's argument was that The Three Pigs' version told for decades was a lie. Counsel Boar went on to say the court's proceedings in the days to come would clear Mr. Wolf's reputation, and send a clear message to would-be accusers that defamation was unacceptable.

"Lies," Counsel Boer contended, "cause hurt, and they will also cost The Three Pigs dearly."

One of the associate counsels for Ms. Priggly, Ms. Sow, made her way to the front of the packed courtroom, pausing sharply before starting her opening argument. Her legs felt weighed down by fear, and her heart galloped like wild horses as she turned and watched the crowd nervously. Ms. Sow felt like she was going into the lion's den. Some of the spectators whispered amongst themselves,

"Why is the incredible Ms. Priggly sending a lightweight into the ring?"

The crowd watched her expectedly as they waited for the return punch in round one of the case of *Mr. Wolf v. The Three Pigs*. Ms. Sow paused, her voice a mere whisper until she felt Ms. Priggly's piercing glare. She finally regained her composure, cleared her throat, and stated boldly and emphatically; "Ladies and gentlemen, we are here to set the record straight and to prove that The Three Pigs' version of the story should be allowed to stand. Everyone knows the story of the crafty old wolf. Let me remind those of you who have forgotten who the victims are in this case. The Three Pigs are the victims in this case of the '*big bad wolf*' versus The Three Little Pigs. Wolves are predators, and predators hunt their prey, just like Mr. Wolf hunted The Three Little Pigs."

Cheers erupted throughout the courthouse as the pigs clapped in agreement. Judge Hognott immediately silenced the cheering audience by banging his gavel, and Ms. Sow continued.

"Members of the jury, we will prove during this trial that the truth is on The Three Pigs' side. Truth is a defense to defamation," with that Ms. Sow trotted to her seat, and sat down.

Ms. Sow looked around the courtroom and smiled, seemingly satisfied with the nods of approval from the pigs, who were pleased with her opening statements. This was her first trial after failing the bar exam numerous times. She had finally passed it on the fourth attempt, and she thought the lines she had rehearsed repeatedly for her opening statement sounded impressive. Ms. Sow prayed for an appearance on the evening news. Even a small story would elevate her stature in the legal community, especially among those who thought she would never become an attorney. Luckily, she had bought a new navy suit with matching pumps for the first day of the trial. One could never look too good for the camera, Ms. Sow thought. While many children wanted to be like Mike, she wanted to be like her aunt, Ms. Priggly. She hoped for once that her aunt, Ms. Priggly, would be proud of her and willing to share the spotlight with her. Ms. Sow visibly relaxed as her aunt smiled at her approvingly before giving her what appeared to be a thumbs up sign.

CHAPTER TWENTY

STRAW HOUSE PIG-THE LAWYER

It was Straw House Pig's turn to present her opening statement. However, Straw House Pig cowered in her seat as her stomach and heart seemed to knot together in fright. She scanned the room briefly, and the disapproving yet confused stares of the many spectators petrified her. The dogs, the foxes, and the wolf clan stood in solidarity. Their menacing icy cold stares seemed to merge into one mighty dagger that pierced through Straw House Pig with the potency of their collective hatred. Straw House Pig closed her eyes, as she tried mentally to block the imaginary hateful growls of the canines in her head. Judge Hognott, quite perturbed at the delay, yelled,

"HURRY UP, MS. STRAW HOUSE PIG, THERE ARE PRESSING COURT MATTERS TO ATTEND TO, SO GET UP AND FACE YOUR ACCUSER."

The Judge's angry outburst immediately jolted Straw House Pig back to the grim reality of the task. She rose timidly from her seat, bending her head in seeming defeat. Her hunched shoulders seemed laden with a heavy burden. The once-nimble feet that pranced about effortlessly as she conducted her daily business now dragged heavily along as if weighed down with iron traps glued to her shoes. She just knew everyone could smell the fear that emanated from her being while the Judge continued to look at her impatiently.

As the minutes ticked by, Straw House Pig remained rooted to the spot, and her voice gave way. Though she attempted to speak, nothing came out of her mouth. To many of the spectators, she looked similar to a stuffed pig going to the proverbial slaughter. Though many of the pigs were angry with her for ruining their chances of winning, a few of them looked at her sympathetically, knowing she was on her own in this fight. It was common knowledge there was bad blood between the sisters. Many focused their anger on Mr. Wolf, who they wished would simply evaporate or disappear off the face of the earth.

"WILL YOU GET STARTED ALREADY?" yelled Judge Hognott as he looked disdainfully at the pig profusely bathed in sweat. *I told this idiot to get an attorney, but she refused*, the Judge thought to himself. *Now she is wasting my time.*

Straw House Pig shook violently with fright and looked at the Judge with hate-filled eyes as she thought he could cut her some slack, considering that she was a novice at this.

"It is now or never," said the Judge as he gave her one long impatient look. The spectators in the courtroom snickered, and some of the wolves howled impatiently. At that moment, the courtroom felt like an inferno to Straw House Pig. The room collapsed into rotating colors as she fell backwards into a crumpled heap in front of the Judge's bench.

Pandemonium ensued as soon as everyone realized the pig was out for the count. Mr. Wolf tried not to laugh at the spectacle and wondered about the camera shots that would appear on TV later in the news. Counsel Boar gave him a stern look that immediately checked any forthcoming snicker. The pig fell flat on her fat rump with her hooves in red shiny pumps high in the air.

"Those pumps seem like a flag of surrender," muttered Samuel Pig to his friend Big Willy.

"Yea," said Big Willy. "Look at those oversized colorful unmentionables hanging loosely around her legs, exposed to this audience and the world tonight on the news."

"Those bloomers are not a pretty sight for anyone to see," replied Samuel Pig.

Judge Hognott was furious at Straw House Pig's meltdown in the courtroom. He looked at the reporters granted access to the courtroom and was dismayed at their obvious glee as they excitedly aimed their cameras on the pig lying on the floor. Judge Hognott raised himself to his full height as he slammed down his gavel and roared,

"RECESS UNTIL FURTHER NOTICE. EVERYONE CLEAR THIS COURTROOM NOW."

Several court officers who seemed to appear out of nowhere sprang into action as they ushered out unwilling patrons who wanted to see this drama unfold. The officers pushed the spectators out of the courtroom as they pressed into others trying to enter into the rapidly emptying courtroom. The officers used their batons and the threat of pepper spray to hold the crowd at bay. The reporters, armed with some of their first shots, tried to find space in the crowded hallways to relay the court happenings via texts. Everyone chatted excitedly as the spectators rehashed the morning events. The Bailiff escorted Ms. Priggly into one of the attorney conference rooms. She fumed as she too digested the scene in the courtroom. She wanted to wrap her hands around stupid Straw House Pig's neck for causing this chaos. Brick House Pig and Stick House Pig sat strangely silent as they pondered the fate of their troubled little sister, whom they had left lying on the courtroom floor. Ms. Priggly knew she had to do some damage control and quickly. She huddled with her associates to strategize her next move.

Meanwhile in the courtroom, Maplewood's EMTs had to wedge their way through the rowdy crowd, and resurrect Straw House Pig from her coma-like faint with the help of some smelling salts. Fifteen minutes later, Straw House Pig slowly opened her eyes, startled by the commotion around her. She peered intently as several pairs of eyes looked down at her unsympathetically. Almost immediately, Straw House Pig remembered why she was lying on the floor. She looked around and noted the courtroom was almost empty, with the exception of the officers and the Judge. The Judge looked at her with clear disgust as he conferred with his law clerk. After asking if she was OK, two EMTs helped Straw House Pig to her feet and seated her on one of the hard court benches. Straw House Pig wished she were anywhere but here in this courtroom, subject to such intense hostility. However, the Judge did not grant Straw House Pig her wish. Judge Hognott looked Straw House Pig directly in her eyes and told her to proceed.

Straw House Pig debated whether she should lie and thought better of it, since the Judge looked as if his all-knowing eyes could see right into her soul. Straw House Pig squeaked out, "I am fine," and before she could finish, Judge Hognott was firing rapid instructions for the court officers to prepare to let the jurors and the spectators back in the courtroom in an orderly fashion. As Straw House Pig gulped down the water given to her, compliments of the Maplewood EMT, she felt slightly better, despite the ordeal she knew was before her. She had just made a fool of herself and she had to redeem her reputation. When the courtroom had filled up again with spectators, the Judge looked at Straw House Pig and said, "We will try this again, Ms. Straw House Pig, and this time please get it right."

Straw House Pig knew all eyes were on her, and she could not afford to fail, so she let out a long breath before she struggled to the front of the courtroom. She avoided all eyes as she stared at the courtroom clock on the wall and recited her lines.

"This is a case of a 'big bad wolf' trying to take revenge on three piglets that embarrassed him years ago," Straw House Pig said as she wrung her hands together and made sure she avoided locking eyes with the evil Mr. Wolf.

She tried to remember the rest of what she practiced, but failed to recollect. Faint rumbling among the patrons in the courtroom registered their disapproval as many wondered yet again, why Judge Hognott had let this dumb pig represent herself. As Straw House Pig struggled to remember her lines, she realized she needed her flash cards. She hurried back to her seat, leaving the audience confused and in limbo as she searched frantically through her big red duffel bag for her notes.

"Where are they?" Straw House Pig muttered as panic overtook her.

She could not believe the cards were not in her bag, and she did not know what to do. Straw House Pig finally placed her two front hooves on her head, since she was standing on her hind legs, and began to stamp and wail quite loudly. The Judge ordered Straw House Pig out of the courtroom until she could control herself. Two court officers carried her out amid her humiliation, to the amusement of many of the spectators.

CHAPTER TWENTY-ONE

DO YOU HAVE A PASS?

own in the lobby of the courthouse, Kourtney created a scene as she tried to enter the courthouse with her dog tucked in her orange Hermes Taurillon Clemence tote bag. As a bark echoed loudly from the bag, the court officer looked at Kourtney incredulously, and told her in a deep booming voice,

"Underage dogs are not allowed in the courthouse unless they are participating in a civil or criminal action."

"Do you know who I am?" Kourtney asked as she stared at the officer defiantly, while her three designer-clad friends flanked her on each side with their faces twisted in surprise.

"I don't care who you are, you will not be entering this courthouse with an underage dog and without a pass," the officer said as he stared at Kourtney with all the disdain he felt. "MY MOTHER IS STICK HOUSE PIG," Kourtney yelled at the officer.

MR. WOLF V. THE THREE PIGS

"I do not care if your mother is the mayor; you are still not getting inside with a dog and without a pass." The officer, already bored with the conversation, moved on to the next person in line.

"I can't believe this idiot will not let me in," Kourtney moaned.

Her three friends looked at her expectantly, waiting for Kourtney to come up with a plan. *They had not donned Prada for nothing*, they thought. Kourtney hurried over to another line, hoping to work her charm on the young officer in charge. Once again, the officer denied them entry. Kourtney's friends glared at her angrily. Kourtney had once again mixed them up in her shenanigans.

CHAPTER TWENTY-TWO

MR. WOLF TAKES THE STAND

Meanwhile in the courtroom, the first person called to the witness stand was the plaintiff, Mr. Wolf. Because this was his big day in court, Mr. Wolf had decided to dress to impress, as he was encouraged to do by Counsel Boar. He wore brown pants and a brown shirt complemented by a beige jacket. He enhanced this look with brown suspenders, a striped brown and beige tie, and a matching handkerchief tucked into his breast pocket. Counsel Boar's opening statement had further boosted his confidence, so Mr. Wolf strutted proudly to the stand, raised his right paw, and promised to tell the truth, and nothing but the truth. However, as he sat in the witness box, his heart began to beat like a marching band. He looked over the audience that seemed to contain everyone from Maplewood and the surrounding towns, as they crammed into the courtroom to listen to his testimony. Mr. Wolf stared at the courtroom clock as he tried to avoid the countless hostile stares.

Mr. Wolf tried to remain focused on his purpose and decided he was not about to let anything spoil his day in court. The cheery smile on his face was quite at odds with the chaos going on inside his head. Additionally, it was out of character for him to wear his heart on his sleeve. The pigs in the courtroom glowered at him menacingly, which reminded him of the long battle ahead. He scanned the audience for some friendly faces, hoping to boost his confidence, and found comfort in the sympathetic looks given to him by Mrs. Wolf, his children, and many of his friends scattered around the courtroom. Mrs. Wolf smiled at him and even blew him a kiss that seemed to float through the air and settle on his brow. He felt a little more at ease and the queasy feeling in his stomach seemed to dissipate. Mr. Wolf fixed his eyes on Mrs. Wolf as if she were his sole means of survival. Noting the distraction, Counsel Boar cleared his throat to get Mr. Wolf's attention and proceeded with his direct examination of his first witness.

"Mr. Wolf, can you please tell the court what happened on the day you first encountered The Three Pigs?" Counsel Boar asked. Mr. Wolf took a deep breath as he faced the court teeming with spectators. He spoke in a loud and clear voice.

"It was a cool but sunny morning, and I was prancing across the meadow trying to catch a yellow butterfly. You know, I was young back then…" He chuckled a bit sheepishly.

"As I looked up the hill, I saw one of Mother Piggy's girls in Papa Fox's apple tree. I ran up the hill shouting as I ran."

"What were you shouting, Mr. Wolf?" asked Counsel Boar, interrupting Mr. Wolf's story.

"I was shouting, 'Stop stealing Papa Fox's apples! Stop stealing Papa Fox's apples! Stop stealing Papa Fox's apples!' When I got up the hill, I stood under the tree pleading with her to stop stealing the apples."

"So what did she say?" Counsel Boar asked.

"She said, 'Shut up! Shut up!'" replied Mr. Wolf, breathing hard as if he were out of breath from a long run.

Counsel Boar looked directly at The Three Pigs and asked that Mr. Wolf identify the pig who told him to "shut up". Mr. Wolf without hesitation pointed directly at Straw House Pig, who was squirming uncomfortably in her seat. Counsel Boar looked directly at the stenographer and around the rest of the courtroom before saying, "For the record, let it be noted that Mr. Wolf pointed at Ms. Straw House Pig as the pig who told him to 'shut up' and was stealing Mr. Fox's apples."

Counsel Boar told Mr. Wolf to continue his story.

"I said to her, 'it is not good to steal,' but Straw House Pig again told me to shut up. To my surprise, she started pelting me with apples, one after the other."

"So you're telling the court, Mr. Wolf," Counsel Boar interjected, "that she was using the apples as dangerous weapons."

"Yes! Yes! She was. I tried dodging the apples, but she hit me pretty badly. I ran down the hill, and I hid behind an avocado tree. She pelted me so badly that I was ducking apples left, right, and center. Every time I peeked out to see if it was clear to make an escape, Straw House Pig would hit me directly in the face with apples."

Judge Hognott barked out a stern "Order! Order! Let there be order in my court!" after the pigs that came out to support The Three Pigs started to laugh as Mr. Wolf recounted his story. The court soon became quiet enough for Mr. Wolf to continue his testimony.

"When I came out, I thought the pig was long gone, so I started walking up the hill. Then a big barrel ran over me, and I was almost flattened. I rolled head first into an avocado tree so hard that the huge green avocadoes fell on my already bruised head and face, causing further excruciating pain."

"Then that *pig*," Mr. Wolf said most forcefully, jumping to his feet and pointing at the pig in pink, jumped out of the barrel and said, 'That's what you get for messing with me.' That heartless pig laughed at my misery, then ran off leaving me crying and wounded. I could not move for a while, so I leaned against a tree, not knowing how I would get home. I was bleeding from my nose, my head, and my feet. Later, a swollen eye and a pounding headache blinded me. In a short while, the weather started to change from bright, sunny to dark, and gloomy. The wind started to blow so hard that I had to find shelter to take care of my wounds. The area was quite desolate, and my only option was to seek help from the very pig who wounded me. I hobbled over to Straw House Pig's residence to ask for help.

"I shouted out to her, 'LITTLE PIG, LITTLE PIG, LET ME COME IN. I FORGIVE YOU, LITTLE PIG. PLEASE! PLEASE! LET ME COME IN. A TORNADO IS COMING.' However, that mean pig shouted, 'NO! NO! NOT BY THE HAIR OF MY CHINNY, CHIN, CHIN, SO YOU MAY AS WELL GO ROT IN HELL.' I was quite embarrassed, but I had to put my pride aside if I wanted to survive this ordeal. Again, I said, 'Little pig, please! Please! I am already hurt, and if you do not let me in, I am going to die out here. Please, little pig, a tornado is coming, let me in.'

She replied, 'No, no, not by the hair of my chinny, chin, chin, you shameless wolf; accept your fate and die in the storm.'

"The mightiest tornado came and blew her house down. I tried holding on to the straw house as I huddled under the eaves, but the wind was too strong," Mr. Wolf said. "She ran away and left me there. I knew her sister's house was stronger, so I went there, limping. I said 'little pig, little pig, the tornado blew away your sister's house. Please let me come in,' but I heard Straw House Pig inside saying again, 'No, no, not by the hair of my chinny, chin, chin.' I said again, 'Please, little pigs, the tornado will kill me. Please, pretty please, let me come in.' but they said not by the hair of their chinny, chin, chin, and the powerful tornado came and blew the house down. All the sticks went flying into the air, and I barely missed a hit in the eye by a sharp stick."

Mr. Wolf paused then said,

"I started to run for my life in the direction both pigs were heading, and that was their big sister's house. It was made of bricks, so I knew that would be my last chance to get a warm place to nurse my wounds. I was limping so badly that I fell down several times. The gale of wind buffeted me so badly that I had to get down on all fours and crawl like a baby to her front door. Upon my arrival, the pigs locked the door, so I knocked on the door, asking Brick House Pig to let me come in. All three replied in a loud chorus, 'Not by the hair of our chinny, chin, chin.' I looked in the distance, and there was another tornado twirling violently toward the house, so I tried getting in through the window, but someone had locked it and boarded it up. I tried climbing onto the roof, shouting, *'LITTLE PIGS, LET ME COME IN.'* They replied 'No, not by the hair of our chinny, chin, chin,' so I climbed into the chimney to escape the tornado."

Counsel Boar asked, "Mr. Wolf, why did you do that?"

Mr. Wolf put his head down as tears streamed from his eyes. He looked so sincere, some of the jurors thought.

Mr. Wolf replied softly, "There was nothing left to do; I would have died if I did not climb down that chimney."

"So what happened next?" Counsel Boar asked.

"As I tried to make my way down the chimney, I was struck by three broomsticks, and The Three Pigs started to poke me all over, which caused me to lose my footing and fall feet first into a big pot of boiling water. I screamed in excruciating pain as the pigs continued to beat me with the broom. 'Please! Please! Please!' I pleaded, 'Do not hurt me.' However, the pigs ignored me. At that moment, Straw House Pig grabbed the pot cover and tried to cover me over in the pot of boiling water. She was the cruelest of the three, and the obscenities that poured from her mouth are just too foul to repeat in this courtroom."

Mr. Wolf became silent, and bent down to pat his feet gently as if reliving the ordeal once again. Mrs. Wolf sobbed pitifully into her handkerchief, breaking the deathly silence that had settled over the courtroom.

After one mournful sigh, Mr. Wolf said, "I still bear the scars today inwardly and outwardly, and only my wife knows the pain and terror I've endured over the years because of that unfortunate encounter."

"So how did you escape?" asked Counsel Boar.

"I do not remember because I was so terrified. I just remember running for my life despite the pain I was feeling. I've never liked pigs since that time."

"Take it easy, Mr. Wolf; remember, I am a pig too," said Counsel Boar with a smirk.

Some of the pigs in the court yelled, "NO YOU'RE NOT!" as they raised their hooves in protest.

"YOU TRAITOROUS PIG!" others yelled angrily at Counsel Boar.

"WOLF LOVER!" one angry pig yelled.

The Judge, furious at these angry outbursts yelled, "ORDER IN THE COURT," as he pounded his gavel and ordered the Bailiff to throw anyone out of the court who continued to be disruptive. Order returned to the courtroom, and the Judge commanded Counsel Boar to proceed.

Counsel Boar then asked Mr. Wolf what happened after he left The Three Pigs. Mr. Wolf sniffled as he recounted how he hopped as fast as he could, eager to get away from the pigs.

"I suffered third-degree burns from falling into the pot of boiling water," Mr. Wolf continued, touching his feet, which still bore the scars of that encounter. "I found shelter in a cave until the storm subsided, and then I painfully hobbled home as best as I could. At home, Mrs. Wolf patched me up with homemade remedies, but the healing process was long, slow, and painful."

"Why didn't you go to the doctor, Mr. Wolf?" Counsel Boar asked.

"I was too embarrassed. I did not want anyone to know that three mischievous pigs had almost killed me. What would my friends think?"

"When was your next encounter with The Three Pigs?"

"My next run-in with The Three Pigs was when they wrote a book called The Three Little Pigs. In the book they lied about how I tried to eat them and how I had blown down the straw house and stick house."

"Did you try to blow down the houses of Straw House Pig and Stick House Pig, Mr. Wolf?"

"I certainly did not," said Mr. Wolf in a most indignant tone.

"So what happened after The Three Pigs wrote this book?"

"Well, I became unwelcome in many places. I was unable to find a job outside of my community, and had to depend on odd jobs and Mrs. Wolf's job at Billy Bog Meat Fest to support the family. Some property owners would not even let me rent an apartment in their neighborhood. I was stuck living out in the woods with my family because I had become the 'big bad wolf' that you often read about in the crime section of the

Daily Read and the *Post*. I could not sleep many nights because the pigs taunted my children as they walked through neighborhoods frequented by pigs. These pigs have damaged my reputation, and my life has been a disaster. The quality of my life has been severely compromised since this unfortunate incident, plain and simple."

Some of the spectators thought they saw tears fall from his eyes, but they could not be sure. Some of the pigs snickered in the back row, glad to see a wolf so vulnerable. Others who were dismayed at the possibility that the jurors would find him believable thought, "*Who is this darn wolf trying to fool with his theatrics? It is obviously just a show to get the jurors' sympathy.*" They hoped the pigs on the jury were not buying this act.

Brick House Pig's attorney, Ms. Priggly, stood up to cross-examine Mr. Wolf, and all heads turned to look at her. She looked the part of a daintily dressed aristocratic pig with an English accent. Dressed in a bright-red power suit, with a white button-down shirt and stiletto heels, Ms. Priggly trotted toward the witness stand with her heels making clicking sounds on the floor. To some of the jurors, it appeared as if Ms. Priggly was strutting on the fashion runway, as her movements were so precise and fluid.

Ms. Priggly was famous in the legal arena for defending P.I.G Insurance Company and Piggy Banks. The city lawyers had accused both companies of lending risky loans, which led to one of the worst recessions in the country. Even the Judge was methodically adjusting his black robe, as if the trial was just getting started. Mr. Wolf curled his tail neatly between his legs as he tried to keep composed as Ms. Priggly walked toward the witness stand. He tried not to appear nervous even though Ms. Priggly looked as if she was heading straight for his jugular. The dainty aristocratic attorney strutted deliberately toward the front of the courtroom, as if she enjoyed making everyone wait. Counsel Boar swallowed hard as he watched Ms. Priggly. She had a reputation in the courts as a legal shark, and it was common knowledge she was not afraid of anything or anybody. Ms. Priggly intimidated witnesses with her glaring stare and twitching snout. Counsel Boar hoped Mr. Wolf would withstand the blistering cross-examination he was sure was afoot.

"Could you please state your name again for the court, Mr. Wolf?" Ms. Priggly asked in her riveting British accent, glancing backward at Mr. Wolf while completing her signature courtroom catwalk.

"My name is Mr. Wolf, as I stated before," stammered Mr. Wolf, looking everywhere but at Ms. Priggly. Mr. Wolf was a little nervous since Ms. Priggly seemed to be going in for the kill.

"Is it really?" asked Ms. Priggly, her English accent appeared more pronounced, and her voice drenched with sarcasm.

"Is it? Well, you will have to excuse me, because I thought it was the '*big bad wolf.*'" Many of the pigs in the courtroom laughed and clapped, and the Judge angrily slammed his gavel on the desk before ordering some of the noisy pigs out of the courtroom.

"OBJECTION!" yelled, Counsel Boar furious with Ms. Priggly's characterization of Mr. Wolf.

"Withdrawn," said Ms. Priggly, looking quite innocently at the Judge and Counsel Boar. The Judge looked at Ms. Priggly as if to reprimand her. He seemed to think better of it, and simply told her to continue with her line of questioning. Counsel Boar was fuming. The Judge was ignoring his objection. It was becoming more and more obvious Ms. Priggly had cast a spell over the Judge. Ms. Priggly quickly fired out her next question.

"Mr. Wolf, on the day in question you said you were just seeking shelter. Is that correct?"

"Yes, that is correct," said Mr. Wolf, looking slightly nervous.

Ms. Priggly smiled before asking Mr. Wolf in an ever-so-sweet voice, "Why would you seek shelter with someone who, according to you, had hurt you so badly, Mr. Wolf?"

"I did because there was no one else around and nowhere else to seek shelter from the tornado."

"Mr. Wolf, do you eat meat?" asked Ms. Priggly.

Counsel Boar interjected, "Objection, Your Honor!"

"On what grounds?" The Judge asked Counsel Boar impatiently.

"On the grounds that Mr. Wolf's answer can be highly prejudicial," offered Counsel Boar.

The Judge seemed to think for a moment before saying in a bored voice, "Overruled. Go ahead; answer the question, Mr. Wolf."

Mr. Wolf cleared his throat and hesitated a bit, then said, "Well… well, no, I do not."

Ms. Priggly then asked, "Do you eat pork, Mr. Wolf?" Mr. Wolf looked at the Judge, the jury, the court officers, Piggy Wiggy's weapon, the other animals in the court, and finally at his attorney, Counsel Boar, who seemed to be waiting like everyone else for an answer.

Suddenly Counsel Boar seemed to recall he was Mr. Wolf's attorney and shouted, "Objection! Your Honor."

"On what basis?" The judge responded sarcastically.

"That question is unduly prejudicial," said Counsel Boar as he glared at Ms. Priggly.

"But it is relevant; it goes to the heart of the question of what Mr. Wolf's intentions were on the day in question," said Ms. Priggly in an authoritative voice. Before the Judge could respond, she tried to move on to her next question, but one female pig in the courtroom shouted out, "Hang that pork eater now!"

"Remove this ill-mannered creature from my courtroom forthwith. Another outburst like this will result in the trial being closed to the public and the media," said the Judge to the Bailiff. "You may continue your line of questioning," said the Judge to Ms. Priggly. Counsel Boar fumed as he scribbled down notes on his yellow legal pad.

"Mr. Wolf, again I ask you, do you eat pork?" asked Ms. Priggly, looking at Mr. Wolf and around the courtroom. Mr. Wolf was now drenched in sweat. He debated whether he should answer the question or not.

"Mr. Wolf, a simple yes or no will suffice," said Ms. Priggly, really enjoying herself. She loved watching Mr. Wolf squirm.

"I am exercising my Fifth Amendment right, so I plead the Fifth," said Mr. Wolf, feeling better for the first time since cross-examination. He had rehearsed this line with Counsel Boar. When he said this, some of the wolves looked around in dismay and the pigs all smiled. Ms. Priggly looked quite satisfied with Mr. Wolf's answer.

She smiled before asking,

"Mr. Wolf, do you know that pigs are trusted to live with humans and their families? Can you say the same for wolves?"

Not giving Mr. Wolf a chance to answer, she proceeded on to her next question.

"Have you ever heard of a hog or a pig killing a wolf?"

"I'm, I'm…no, I can't say I have," stammered Mr. Wolf, once again feeling quite nervous, "but I almost got killed by three of them sitting right here in the courtroom." Some of the spectators' loud snickers upset the quiet of the courtroom as they took great pleasure in Mr. Wolf's discomfort.

Ms. Priggly, hand on her hips, fixed a cold intimidating stare on Mr. Wolf and asked, "Mr. Wolf, who would you say is more dangerous, a pig or a wolf?"

Mr. Wolf felt trapped and did not know how to respond to Ms. Priggly. He nervously wiped beads of sweat from his face, got up from his seat, and stood with his paws wide apart before answering the question.

"What's the matter? Do you need more time to answer the question?" Ms. Priggly asked her voice drenched in sarcasm.

Before Mr. Wolf could answer, Ms. Priggly said,

"Do you know what I think, Mr. Wolf? I think you were trying to outsmart and kill those Three Little Pigs; instead, they outsmarted you and nearly did to you what you were trying to do to them, which was to make a meal out of them. However, you could not tell Mrs. Wolf the true story of how you were nearly cooked alive by *The Three Little Pigs* after you tried to break into their house, could you, Mr. Wolf?" shouted Ms. Priggly. "Instead, you chose to lie. You are not here to clear your name, Mr. Wolf. You are here to clear your shame."

"No! No! That is not true, you lying pig! How would you know when you were not even there?" shouted Mr. Wolf. Ms. Priggly just stared at him, looking quite amused.

Counsel Boar jumped to his feet, breaking the silence with a thunderous, "Objection! Objection, I say!"

"On what grounds?" Judge Hognott stared at both lawyers as he asked his question.

"Ms. Priggly is badgering the witness," said Counsel Boar. Ms. Priggly threw up both front hooves while looking down at the floor thoughtfully. She walked over to the defense's table and took a sip from her cup of water before continuing her attack on Mr. Wolf while everyone waited eagerly.

Ms. Priggly returned to the witness box, wrinkled her brow, and looked threateningly at Mr. Wolf.

"So you are telling us, and you want the court to believe, you were not looking to make a meal out of *The Three Little Pigs*, Mr. Wolf?"

"No, I was not," replied Mr. Wolf loudly after clearing his throat. "Many of you may not know this, but I am a vegan."

Ms. Priggly almost yelled, "A what, Mr. Wolf?" clearly in disbelief.

"A vegan, I eat no meat, no bacon, no snout, no curd, no nothing, nada,"

Mr. Wolf said, gesticulating with his right front paw, suddenly feeling very sure of himself. He watched with satisfaction as Ms. Priggly stared at him with utter disgust. For the first time, the formidable Ms. Priggly looked visibly shaken and shortly covered her snout with her right front hoof. Mr. Wolf's answer had startled her.

"No more questions at this time, Your Honor. But we reserve the right to call Mr. Wolf to the stand again."

Ms. Priggly knew that she had to check out this tall tale, and beat Mr. Wolf and his attorney at whatever game they were playing. The Three Pigs, sitting in the courtroom, all turned a bright shade of red as they listened to Mr. Wolf's responses.

Mr. Wolf's tangle with the she-pig was over. He felt as if he had survived the lion's den intact. He sat in the witness stand with his head slightly bowed; still reeling from Ms. Priggly's blistering cross-examination. Inwardly, Mr. Wolf smiled as he recognized he had made a direct hit on the ego of the formidable, unflappable Ms. Priggly.

The courtroom was spinning with excitement after Mr. Wolf's testimony. Since the Judge prohibited texting in the courtroom, reporters were furiously jotting down notes. Spectators exchanged whispers and scribbled notes away from the watchful eye of the court officers who tried to maintain order in the courtroom. One or two fearless spectators had been able to snap pictures of Mr. Wolf on the witness stand with phones they had snuck into the courtroom. The court officer caught one offender and immediately kicked her out of the courtroom. The court officer fumed at the idea that someone was sleeping on the job and allowed the phone to be smuggled into the courtroom. He made a note to confront the incompetent later.

It was Straw House Pig's turn to cross-examine Mr. Wolf, and she had one question to ask this devious old wolf. After giving herself a pep talk for over an hour, Straw House Pig was ready to face this wolf. Straw House Pig approached the witness stand, glad she had taken the time to put on her shaded glasses. She looked Mr. Wolf directly in his eyes through shades and asked in a high, squeaky voice,

"Can you please point out the characters in this courtroom who you stated earlier attacked you, Mr. Wolf, on the day in question?"

Mr. Wolf, flabbergasted by the audacity of this pesky pig to question him, yelled loudly, "IT WAS YOU, YOU IDIOT!"

Straw House Pig raced back to her seat, frightened that the wolf was about to attack her. The courtroom erupted into laughter before Judge Hognott silenced Mr. Wolf and the spectators with a stern look. Mr. Wolf counted to three, upset that he had let this darn pig see him rattled. Ms. Priggly tried to shake off the headache that was threatening to overtake her as she observed Straw House Pig. She would definitely have to have a talk with that troublesome pig. Counsel Boar smiled; it appeared this trial was already full of surprises.

CHAPTER TWENTY-THREE

MR. FOX TO THE RESCUE

Counsel Boar called Mr. Fox to the witness stand. Mr. Fox was dressed in a red overall, with a plaid shirt and dirt-caked yellow rain boots. Mr. Fox's reddish-brown fur, red handlebar mustache, and bushy beard made him an odd figure in the courtroom. He took his assigned seat before delving into his testimony. Counsel Boar asked Mr. Fox about his relationship with The Three Pigs.

"I have no problem with all the pigs in the case, just Straw House Pig," Mr. Fox replied.

"Why?" Counsel Boar asked.

"Every season just before I could pick my apples for market, she would sneak onto my farm, climb my apple tree, and load up her wheelbarrow with my apples. That is why."

"Do you have this problem with all pigs?"

"No," Mr. Fox replied. "It is only with bush pigs such as Straw House Pig who steal farmers' crops and cause great financial loss and distress."

"Now, Mr. Fox, can you tell us how Mr. Wolf got caught up in this confusion between Straw House Pig and yourself?"

"Well, Mr. Wolf only tried to help me when he saw that thieving good-for-nothing pig trying to take my apples,"

Mr. Fox said, looking directly at Straw House Pig, who was fiddling with papers in the front row, seemingly oblivious to the accusations being hurled her way.

Counsel Boar asked Mr. Fox, "Why didn't you say something to help Mr. Wolf all these years?"

"I tried to say something, but no one wanted to hear the facts. Everyone seemed to like the sensationalized version of the story of three helpless little pigs attacked by the 'big bad wolf' better. I reported the matter to Sheriff Hogbottom countless times, but he told me I had better have some evidence before making these accusations about Momma Piggy's fine young girl. I felt so intimidated every time I reported an incident about the pigs to the sheriff because he would often come with his deputies, who had their shotguns drawn as I gave my report. On one occasion, Sheriff Hogbottom even tore up my report and said, 'This is what I think of your report. Its rubbish,' as he stepped on it. Furthermore, Sheriff Hogbottom was always giving me tickets for frivolous violations he said were quite apparent on the farm. I believe he gave me those tickets to intimidate and shut me up. What could I do? I live in a county overrun by pigs, so I did what any sensible fox would do and kept my mouth shut. In addition to that, I could barely understand what Sheriff Hogbottom was saying most of the time. He was always speaking in that Pig Latin language," said Mr. Fox with some disdain. Mr. Fox did not have much use for country pigs, who he thought were too stuck in their ways and cultural language. Some of the pigs in the courtroom booed Mr. Fox because they felt he was making fun of pigs. The Judge immediately silenced them with his gavel.

"Thank you. No further questions, Mr. Fox," said Counsel Boar, seemingly satisfied with the direct examination of Mr. Fox.

On cross-examination, Ms. Priggly asked, "Aren't you part of the Canidae family, Mr. Fox?"

"Objection!" shouted Counsel Boar.

"On what grounds?" The Judge asked Counsel Boar his impatience rapidly increasing.

"Relevancy—what does Mr. Fox's genes have to do with anything?" Counsel Boar asked.

The Judge looked at Ms. Priggly, waiting for her to supply the answer. "I want to show bias, Your Honor," Ms. Priggly said ever so sweetly as she stared at both the Judge and Counsel Boar.

"Objection overruled!" said the Judge. "You may proceed with your line of questioning," he told Ms. Priggly. She again asked Mr. Fox, "Are you from the Canidae family?"

"Yes I am," Mr. Fox said, beaming proudly. Ms. Priggly smiled triumphantly and said excitedly, "No further questions, Your Honor."

Mr. Fox suddenly stopped smiling when he realized the implications of what Ms. Priggly had asked.

Straw House Pig, after watching Ms. Priggly's performance, felt more courageous as she pranced to the front of the courtroom, ready to confront Mr. Fox.

If that pig can do it, I can do it too, Straw House Pig thought.

"Mr. Fox, do you have any evidence that Straw House Pig was the one stealing your apples?" she asked, referring to herself in the third person.

"Do you have any pictures of this Straw House Pig eating your apples?

I mean, everybody knows foxes are known for being sly, aren't they, Mr. Fox, SO YOU MUST BE MAKING ALL THIS STUFF UP TO HELP MR. WOLF, YOUR BUDDY, AREN'T YOU?" Straw House Pig yelled at the top of her lungs, shattering the momentary quietude in the courtroom.

Mr. Fox looked ready to burst a blood vessel, as the veins in his neck seemed to bulge dangerously. Straw House Pig had her hands on her hips with her big mouth agape as she badgered him with questions in a shrill voice.

By then, Judge Hognott was irritated. Straw House Pig's annoying high-pitched voice drowned out most of her words. The Judge soon halted the questioning, much to the relief of Mr. Fox as he left the witness stand giving Straw House Pig a hateful look. Straw House Pig felt elated because she felt she had touched a raw nerve and scored high points in her questioning of Mr. Fox. She almost tripped on her own hooves as she cockily walked back to her seat, once again becoming the center of hysterical laughter. Judge Hognott was tired and had had enough of Straw House Pig's shenanigans, so he calmly said,

"We will recess until tomorrow at 9:00 a.m., and tomorrow, we will have some decorum in this court, or I will not hesitate to throw out anyone who is a distraction."

He looked directly at Straw House Pig, who was now red in the face with embarrassment, and anxious to get out of the courtroom. Straw House Pig could feel Brick House Pig's disdainful glare at her, but for once, she did not care what anyone thought of her. Straw House Pig turned around and stuck out her tongue at her sister.

"Take that, you stuck-up pig," Straw House Pig whispered as she clutched her bag and tried to merge with the crowd, trying to escape from the courtroom with some dignity intact.

As she walked down the courthouse steps swaddled in her pink polyester jacket, reporters mobbed Straw House Pig. She felt like a celebrity as the camera lenses and microphones slammed into her face. She watched as the famous Ms. Priggly kept giving her the poison eye. Watch me and weep, Straw House Pig thought as she posed for the camera, hardly aware of the jokes made at her expense.

CHAPTER TWENTY-FOUR

AMBUSHED

When Mr. Wolf left court that day, he was visibly upset. However, the long walk home gave him the chance to cool down. The sun had set, so the intense heat had cooled even though the air was still quite humid. Mr. Wolf slapped away the buzzing bees that sailed past his ears as he walked the last mile to his house. As he neared home, he was most shocked to see throngs of reporters camped around his abode. He tried to contain his anger when some of them snapped his picture and shoved microphones in his face. They fired off questions one after the other and one reporter yelled,

"What was it like to face the formidable Ms. Priggly?" Another shouted,

"Do you really expect us to believe that you are a vegan, Mr. Wolf?"

"Must I always be the butt of jokes among my tormentors?" he asked.

"Over the years, I've managed to stay clear of a decadent society that has alienated me from their foul presence, but today, they are here to rob me of the peace that I cherish dearly. Their presence here is a constant reminder of my wasted life and stolen ambitions. I guess it's a cross I must bear," Mr. Wolf said aloud angrily as he pushed past a reporter, whose question generated peals of laughter among the many reporters who invaded the sanctity of the dense forest.

The reporter had asked loudly "Did you try to eat those pigs Mr. Wolf" as he elbowed his fellow reporters.

The noise of the few dozen reporters had desecrated the peaceful environment that shielded Mr. Wolf from the scorn and derision of a hateful world. He stared ahead as he hurried past a reporter who was furiously trying to scribble down his comments.

Mr. Wolf's neighbors, annoyed by all the commotion in their relatively quiet community, yelled at the reporters to go away.

One angry dog barked, "Go harass The Three Pigs and leave us alone."

One reporter tried to grab Mr. Wolf as he hurried to his front door and pleaded,

"Please, Mr. Wolf, just one comment."

Mr. Wolf faked a smile and said, "Next time" as he opened his door and slammed it tightly shut, glad to shut out the insanity that invaded his privacy.

"It has been like this all evening," Mrs. Wolf complained as she peered out the window, quite weary of the noise surrounding their outer sanctuary.

"I hope this is worth it, Wolfie," Mrs. Wolf said as she closed back the drapes and faced him with her paws akimbo.

Mr. Wolf was too tired to answer Mrs. Wolf. Instead, he walked to the television set and turned the knob. The black-and-white floor model TV was quite fuzzy, so he frequently moved the hanger around that had long since replaced the antenna as he tried to get a better reception. He needed to watch the nightly news to see the spin on the case. Finally, the reception was clear enough for him to see the news. He sat on his old black-and-white checkered sofa to watch the evening news. Mr. Wolf pulled off his brown shoes and black smelly socks, and then rested his tired feet on the center table, eager to relax after a hard day of mental abuse. Mrs. Wolf watched him intently, quite exasperated with the way The Three Pigs had disrupted their lives. Mr. Wolf avoided her accusing stare as he listened to the media out take from the court. Mrs. Wolf, quite fed up with his seeming indifference, yelled to Mr. Wolf, "DINNER IS ALMOST READY," as she stomped into the kitchen.

CHAPTER TWENTY-FIVE

THE MEDIA SPEAKS

It was Straw House Pig, some argued, who was doing the best without the advice of counsel. People who had never been excited about the news raced home to watch it with their families. Others hung out with friends in public spaces just to chat about the first day's happenings of *Mr. Wolf v. The Three Pigs*. The news stories that evening revolved around the first day of the trial. The late edition of the evening papers such as the *Maplewood Gazette* carried pictures of Straw House Pig flat on her back on the hard courtroom floor. One news caption in the *Maplewood Post* titled in bold read, "**Straw House Pig Lies on Her Back on the First Day of Court.**" In the *Maplewood Daily* it read in bold, "**Down for the Count: Fool for a Lawyer**" above a picture of Straw House Pig running from Mr. Wolf. The Associated Press wired the news of the trial of *Mr. Wolf v. The Three Pigs* around the globe. Peals of hysterical laughter filled the air around Maplewood at dinner tables, in sports clubs, and in every public business place imaginable. The courtroom fiasco of Straw House Pig as described by news commentators became fodder for comics everywhere. Some criticized the Judge for allowing her to make a mockery of the court system, while others lamented the high cost of greedy attorneys who refused to defend Straw House Pig, thus leaving her to fend for herself. Others discussed the limitation of the Sixth Amendment's right to counsel as it related only to the accused in criminal cases.

The news stations that evening crammed their programs with commentaries about the first day of the trial of *Mr. Wolf v. The Three Pigs*. Many of the commentators mentioned how amazed they were that so many people had attended the trial.

"This is the trial of the century," one historian commented as he gave a history of other noteworthy trials.

One of the commentators from a reputable university well versed in courtroom proceedings argued that for the first time in Maplewood, spectators had turned out in record numbers for a trial. Fox News commentators argued that Mr. Wolf did a superb job on the witness stand. Furthermore, it was a brilliant strategy for Counsel Boar to call him as the first witness, thus setting the stage to destroy a long entrenched lie. CNN commentators summarized the day's happenings in court, while some of the commentators on MSNBC argued that Ms. Priggly hammered Mr. Wolf on the witness stand. They particularly liked the fact that she fiercely challenged his story about being afraid of the pigs when in fact the pigs had every right to be afraid of him.

Meanwhile, on Fox 5, they applauded Mr. Fox for supporting Mr. Wolf's story. Additionally, the Fox News commentators brought in Ms. Foxology, an anthropologist, to talk about bush pigs. Mr. Fox had claimed that Straw House Pig was a bush pig. Ms. Foxology was a reed-thin fox with wild curly red hair tamed by a brown barrette. She wore red square-framed glasses that gave her a nerdy look. She was dressed in a well-worn white T-shirt that read, "Save the Trees." Her blue faded jeans and dirty white high - top sneakers completed her outfit. Ms. Foxology face was devoid of makeup, but her reddish cheeks radiated good health. She exuded an excited energy about her job as an anthropologist that seemed almost contagious. Fresh from a trip to the Amazon Forest, the anthropologist talked passionately about the construct of the bush pig.

"Bush pigs are known to be pests on agricultural land mostly because they love fruits," she said.

"Wouldn't this characterization support Mr. Wolf and Mr. Fox's contention that the Straw House Pig had been trying to steal their apples?" asked the commentator.

"Yes, based on my research, bush pigs find apples irresistible, so it is quite plausible that Straw House Pig could have been taking the apples from Mr. Fox's tree," Ms. Foxology continued excitedly, her eyes shining like stars as she beamed into the camera.

Simultaneously, on MSNBC, Ms. Meadow was arguing that Ms. Priggly got in a good zinger when she asked Mr. Fox if he was part of the Canidae family on cross-examination.

"We all know the Canidae will always stick together, and since the wolf, the fox, and the dog are all related, it would only make sense that Mr. Fox would lie for Mr. Wolf," Ms. Meadow said in her usual commentary-style diatribe. She then launched into the history of the Canidae family for the viewers who were unaware of this genealogical connection. Thousands of pigs e-mailed her in agreement.

Mr. Wolf was missing all that was occurring on the cable networks since he did not have cable. Instead, he watched the nightly news. He rose from his seat repeatedly to switch the channels between two, four, seven, and nine as he wrestled with the hanger to get a clear picture. Mr. Wolf now wished he had listened to his children when they had urged him to get with the times and buy a new TV, get cable, and a remote control. Eventually he successfully switched to channel nine to a breaking news story.

"It has been confirmed that a pig is the latest victim of wolf aggression," the news anchor reported. "The wolf attacked the pig as he was on his way to work earlier this morning. Luckily, a passing pig rescued the victim from the jaws of the wolf, who has been preying on unsuspecting victims for the past month. Unfortunately, the pig succumbed to his wounds on the way to the hospital, while the wolf was caught in the act and taken into custody by the authorities."

Mr. Wolf groaned wearily.

"Why now?" he asked.

"This is just what the media needs to vilify the wolf community, and I hope they will not link this story to my case."

Later that night, Mr. Wolf ate the last of his dessert, consisting of cake and custard, while sitting around his small circular dinner table made out of bamboo with matching seating for two. He lingered at the dinner table, and slowly dabbed his mouth with his napkin, seemingly lost in deep thought. The broken toothpick that stuck carelessly at the corner of his mouth fell to the floor, and he retrieved another from the pack in the middle of the table. By then Mrs.Wolf had long finished her meal and excused herself to wash the dinnerware. As she was watching her sugar intake, she had decided against dessert. Mrs. Wolf had most of the dinnerware cleared from the table and after dipping them in warm water, she was now painstakingly licking the dishes clean. Her long pink tongue methodically swept the smooth surface of each plate until it was sparkling. Mr. Wolf looked at her admiringly. As Mrs. Wolf appeared unusually quiet, Mr. Wolf wondered if he should bring up the trial, since the conversation at the dinner table had been void of any court talk.

After Mrs. Wolf licked the last plate clean, Mr. Wolf asked,

"Can you believe that stuck-up old maid of a pig asked me whether a wolf was more dangerous than a pig? Can you believe her stupidity in saying that pigs are so non-violent that they live with humans as if that is such a good thing? Doesn't she know that pigs have more to fear from human beings than from wolves? On Christmas Day, human beings just love to eat that hog meat. Matter of fact, almost every morning humans are filling their bellies with bacon. I wonder if that dumb pig knows bacon is pork. But then again, she probably does not read the ingredients, since she is too busy studying ways to trap poor defenseless creatures on that witness stand," said Mr. Wolf as he laughed for the very first time that day. "Well, I just love being a wolf since most humans are not exactly lining up to eat my meat."

Mrs. Wolf listened in silence as he continued his rant. "One time I passed Old McDonald's farm and saw over five hundred pigs in that pen," said Mr. Wolf, laughing in a loud raspy voice. "When they spotted me, Old McDonald told his farm helps to get that wolf, so they chased me off the farm. Now with all her intelligence, you would think Ms. Priggly would know why Old McDonald was raising all those pigs."

"Well, Wolfie, you were adamant about clearing your name; therefore, you have to put up with this nonsense," said Mrs. Wolf, finally speaking as she furiously scrubbed a burned pot and breaking one of her long red nails in the process.

Mrs. Wolf gave Mr. Wolf a chilling look and said, "I watched you in court as you sat there answering those idiotic questions that prissy pig was firing at you while that judge, another pig, told her to proceed with her questions." She was clearly angry about the events in court that day, which she told her husband was nothing but a farce.

"Mr. Wolf, it seemed to me that you were the one on trial today and not the three stupid pigs," Mrs. Wolf continued angrily as she dried the last of her dishes with a dishcloth and put them in the cupboard. She wiped her wet paws on her apron as she turned to face Mr. Wolf.

"On the contrary, I think things are going rather splendid," said Mr. Wolf as he cleaned his teeth with a toothpick and let out a loud belch. Mrs. Wolf was used to Mr. Wolf's bad manners, so she ignored him as she continued her tirade.

"I can bet my next retirement check that sassy pig is not married, because I can't see how anyone, not even a darn pig, could put up with her highfaluting ways. Furthermore, I bet you if I caught her high and mighty hinny outside of that courtroom that her hooves could not move as fast as her mouth," howled Mrs. Wolf in a low gravelly voice, wrinkling her brow.

Mr. Wolf howled even more menacingly at Mrs. Wolf's remarks, happy that she had regained some of her humor since dinner had been an icy and quiet affair.

"Be kind now, Mrs. Wolf; all this talk is not good for your blood pressure. Furthermore, this whole thing will end soon, and the whole world is going to know the truth. The fact is that I did not blow their houses down, and I did not try to eat those silly pigs." Mr. Wolf yawned, quite exhausted from the day's proceedings.

He stood up, patted his stomach before grabbing Mrs. Wolf's paws, and spun her around the kitchen playfully as they recalled the antics of Straw House Pig. Mrs. Wolf smiled as he turned on the gramophone, dimmed the lights, and grabbed her around her slender waist. He held her in a gentle embrace and led her in an up-tempo fox trot across the small kitchen floor to the beat of "King of the Forest, Queen of My Heart." They rocked rhythmically to the thumping beat while laughing hysterically like little children. In the heat of their romp, they reminisced about their young and carefree days. Mr. Wolf was determined to savor the light moment and forget about the awful incident with the pigs that had stolen his joy and consumed every waking moment of their lives.

Mrs. Wolf laughed loudly and said,

"Goodness, Wolfie! You still have your spunk!"

Finally, out of breath, they collapsed on the couch, laughing playfully. Mrs. Wolf looked at her husband and sighed. She secretly longed for happier times when her Wolfie was not carrying the weight of the world on his shoulders. Mr. Wolf could sometimes be so adorable despite his other irritating ways. She smiled sweetly and thought, *ah, yes, I really do love this old wolf. He is the love of my life, and the joy of my existence.* As if reading her thoughts, Mr. Wolf leaned over and planted a big wet sloppy kiss on her forehead, and they both laughed uproariously. Now tired and exhausted, they trotted off to bed for a good night's sleep.

CHAPTER TWENTY-SIX

THE SHERIFF COMES TO TOWN

The next day Counsel Boar called Sheriff Hogbottom to the witness stand. He was dressed in his full sheriff regalia, with the addition of his big boots and western hat. This commanding figure of a pig strutted into the courtroom with a confidence that held the audience spellbound. The courtroom became deadly quiet as Sheriff Hogbottom took a seat on the witness stand. His reflective glasses made it impossible to see his eyes. Sheriff Hogbottom took his time removing his glasses. When seated, he surveyed the courtroom as if he were taking a mental inventory of each occupant. Sheriff Hogbottom squinted lazily, and then steadfastly fixated his gaze on Counsel Boar disdainfully. The Judge looked down at Sheriff Hogbottom with some displeasure, and requested sternly that he remove his hat.

Counsel Boar approached the witness stand and said with a smile on his face, "How are you doing this morning, Sheriff Hogbottom?" The sheriff took his time before answering in a slow drawl that many referred to as Country Pig Latin.

"I guess I can say ama doin' none too kindly as I had to leave my fine job to comea to this herea courthouse," said Sheriff Hogbottom. Counsel Boar looked a bit puzzled as he tried to decipher Sheriff Hogbottom's response. He attempted again to question him.

"So, Sheriff Hogbottom, how many times were you called by Mr. Fox to deal with the pigs?" asked Counsel Boar.

Sheriff Hogbottom squinted and stared at Counsel Boar hard before answering, "I wouda say about two or three a time."

"Did you take a report?" Counsel Boar asked.

"I woulda reckon I did, sincesa that a part a ma joba." Sheriff Hogbottom had an almost sinister look on his face.

"So what did your report say?"

"The report said just what it was a supposa to say, which was that there was a fox astirring up trouble in our necks a the woods and trying to cause somea trouble on Mother Piggy's fine yungans," said Sheriff Hogbottom. "Three fine piglets Mother Piggy did raise, they mighty fine. Ah known dem since they were borna, and here come some slya old fox stirring up trouble."

"So, Sheriff Hogbottom, you are saying you did not investigate the claims that Farmer Fox told you about?" asked Counsel Boar in an incredulous voice.

During Sheriff Hogbottom's testimony, the court stenographer sent a message to the Judge stating that Sheriff Hogbottom needed an interpreter because she found it difficult to understand him. The court recessed for an hour while they located a pig well versed in Country Pig Latin to interpret.

Once the interpreter was in place, Counsel Boar resumed questioning Sheriff Hogbottom.

"Did you investigate Farmer Fox's complaint about the pig?" he asked.

Sheriff Hogbottom, looking at Counsel Boar as if he were dim-witted, and then continued. "What wasa therea to investigatea? It was kinda obvious that the foxa was a lyin sincesa I asked hima about how manya applea he dida hava ona that treea, and that old lyinga fox could not a tell mea how manya apple he hada thata dear treea. It was obvious that we hadda a sly fox telling talla tales on upright citizens of our fine town," said Sheriff Hogbottom, drawing out his words. "We not lika you city folks. We don't eat our youngas, we protecta them. Looka ata youa, Counsel Boar, putting on airsa and forgottena where ya a come froma. Your kina folks must be so troubled to see howa you turned out defending some wolf. I hopa there is a special placa for pigs lika ya." Sherriff Hogbottom continued to look at Counsel Boar with utmost contempt while chewing what appeared to be gum.

The blogosphere went crazy after Sheriff Hogbottom's testimony. Everyone thought the sheriff was hilarious. One website called wolfsideofthestory.com blogged that it was obvious wolves could not get a fair chance in towns where pigs overran the legal system. "Sheriff Hogbottom," one blogosphere wrote, "Is a typical example of the trouble with the legal system in this part of the country." John Stewart, a comedian known for his political satire, dressed up like Sheriff Hogbottom and poked fun at the Sheriff. He spoke in a dialect similar to the one the Sheriff had used on the witness stand. The caption at the bottom of the television screen translated what John Stewart was saying. This particular episode was soon seen all over the world, posted to YouTube and Facebook, and discussed on all the news outlets. *The Daily Show with John Stewart* had never seen ratings like this.

CHAPTER TWENTY-SEVEN

WEATHER PIG TAKES THE STAND

Next, Counsel Boar called Whistle Pig, the well-respected groundhog, to the stand. Whistle Pig was to testify about the weather on the day of the incident. Whistle Pig was a disheveled brownish-grey groundhog with two oversized protruding teeth. The large red glasses he wore seemed to consume his face. He was dressed in an old threadbare grey jacket that had obviously seen better days and matching grey high-water slacks. Due to his advanced age and slow gait, the groundhog seemed to take only one-step every hour. When Whistle Pig finally sat down, he seemed lost behind the large desk, so Officer Piggy Wiggy propped him up on a high chair.

"State your name and occupation for the court," Counsel Boar said.

"Well, yes, my name is Whistle Pig, also known as the groundhog in charge of forecasts and weather records for all the country, North, East, South, and West…"

"OK, OK," the Judge interrupted impatiently. "Counsel Boar, please proceed with your questions."

"What was the weather like on that famous day in question?" Counsel Boar asked so as not to invoke the Judge's displeasure. Whistle Pig, taken aback by the Judge's impatience, looked over his shoulder after peeping over his glasses at Judge Hognott. He leafed through a stack of papers that seemed to have a gazillion pages at an even more painfully slow rate. The papers, already a dirty-looking yellowish color, seemed to age as Whistle Pig leafed through them.

Mr. Whistle Pig seemed quite oblivious to the audience's impatient sighs and groans of exasperation as they awaited his answer while he searched through his stack of papers. About ten minutes later, he picked out a sheet of paper and looked at it for another ten minutes. In fact, Whistle Pig seemed a bit hesitant before he squeaked out his reply in a barely audible voice.

"According to my notes, there was a tornado in that vicinity on the day in question." Pandemonium broke loose in the courtroom as the pigs and their supporters jumped out of their seats, howling and squeaking loudly. One bold pig to the left side of the courtroom, red in the face with anger, shook his front right hoof at Whistle Pig and shouted, "SILENCE THAT JUDAS FAKE PIG ON THE STAND!" The Judge had to summon more court officers for Whistle Pig's safety. Whistle Pig was now shaking furiously with fright.

"Is there anything else you remember about the day in question, Mr. Whistle Pig?" asked Counsel Boar in a calm and gentle voice, because he did not want to frighten Whistle Pig any further.

Mr. Whistle Pig hesitated and taking a deep breath, stated, "I distinctly remember the day in question. All the groundhogs at the weather bureau were quite busy sending out the whistle alarm to alert the community that there was a strange depression brewing in the region."

"No further questions," Counsel Boar said, satisfied with Whistle Pig's testimony.

When it was Ms. Priggly's turn to cross-examine Mr. Whistle Pig, she looked at him with all the contempt she could muster and asked,

"Was the alarm you mentioned on the day in question specifically signaling a tornado, Mr. Whistle Pig, since you did not say?"

Mr. Whistle Pig seemed to shrink in size as he cowered nervously under Ms. Priggly's withering glare. "No, since our alarm equipment was not working well that day, but it did appear to be a tornado," stuttered Whistle Pig, anxious to get off the witness stand and away from this mean English pig.

"Mr. Whistle Pig, can you tell us who certified the report your read earlier?" asked Ms. Priggly. She strolled over to stand closer to the jurors and smiled at them as if they were all in cahoots.

"I did," said Whistle Pig haltingly. Ms. Priggly scanned the jurors as they took in Mr. Whistle Pig's answer.

"No further questions," she said, waving her hoof daintily as if in triumph and strutting back to her seat. Straw House Pig decided not to cross-examine Whistle Pig.

Whistle Pig was immediately ushered out of the courtroom for his safety as two pigs raised signs reading, "**Kill the Traitor.**" The Judge had both pigs handcuffed and removed from the courtroom as other pigs booed their removal. The wolves and the foxes cheered as the court officers forcibly collared and dumped the pigs outside the courthouse. The disruptive pigs, on the other hand, ranted wildly as the guards led them away. Some cows present in the courtroom watched in disbelief at the unfolding courtroom soap opera.

"Boy am I glad that we do not have a stake in this contentious spectacle," a plump heifer sitting in the back row mooed softly.

Judge Hognott finally brought the courtroom under control, having broken his gavel on his podium. He warned, "If there is another outburst like this in this courtroom, everyone, including the media, will be thrown out immediately." He then requested another gavel.

Later that evening, the blogosphere was buzzing with activity as comments rapidly posted from around the globe in response to what had happened in court that day. Some of the commentators made wisecracks about Whistle Pig's damning testimony and his slowness. Several spectators claimed they had fallen asleep while he testified due to the sweltering heat in the packed courtroom and the groundhog's monotonous discourse.

News commentators on their respective programs brought in meteorologists to discuss weather conditions on the day the wolf had encountered The Three Little Pigs. Some meteorologists stated that they recalled heavy rain during that period, but they were not sure if an actual tornado had occurred. On Fox News, the groundhog put in an appearance. He once again reiterated what he had said in court about the weather conditions. He also spoke about the chilling glares directed at him by the pigs in the courtroom and their outright lack of respect for law and order.

"It's a proven fact that 'truth' is strictly subjective for that faction of society," he said. "They have absolutely no interest in the truth of the matter."

Once again, the commentators on Fox News chimed in on the intimidating tactics the pigs were using, such as packing the courtroom with more pigs and not allowing enough wolves into the court to watch the trial. One commentator claimed,

"This is what happens when you let one group control the court system."

Fox News encouraged more wolves to go to court and support Mr. Wolf.

CHAPTER TWENTY-EIGHT

MOTHER PIG ORDERED TO COURT

COURT OF MAPLEWOOD
CIVIL COURT
--x
MR. WOLF

                 Plaintiff,

Vs.   Index Number: 12345

BRICK HOUSE PIG
STRAW HOUSE PIG
STICK HOUSE PIG

                 Defendants.

--x

Subpoena for Appearance in a Civil Case

To: **Mother Pig**, resident of 333 Hogwood Lane, Maplewood:

You are Ordered by the Court to appear at the Civil Court of Maplewood on August 15, of This Year at 10:00 a.m., 2nd Floor Courtroom, regarding the matter of Mr. Wolf v. The Three Pigs, Index Number: 12345, and to testify and to remain until excused.

NOTICE

This Subpoena is issued pursuant to Maplewood Civil Code 107. If you fail to attend, you may be subject to sanctions including, but not limited, to imprisonment and attorney's fees.

Inquiries concerning this subpoena should be Addressed to: Law Offices of Honest Pig and Honest Pig
Attention: Counsel Boar
6 Maplewood Lane
Telephone Number: 555-555-1212
Fax Number: 555-555-2121

Witness the Honorable Judge Hognott of the Civil Court of Maplewood.
By the Court:
Clerk of Civil Court

Counsel Boar subpoenaed Mother Pig to testify for the Plaintiff's case in chief. Mother Pig took the stand. Her salt and pepper hair drawn back from her face in a French roll with the wire-framed glasses perched on her snout gave her an air of sophistication. The neatly pressed black polyester dress was tight around her midriff, and appeared to have seen better days. As she haltingly approached the witness stand, her well-polished black pleather flats made loud squeaking sounds. For more than thirty years, Mother Pig had worked a sixteen-hour workday as a server at the Forever Open Diner, and her calloused hooves still hurt painfully. As she settled in her seat on the witness stand, she proudly set her black and white Prada pocketbook on her lap. This was the most prized among her many handbags because it was a birthday gift from her oldest daughter, Brick House Pig. *I wish I did not have to testify against my own children, but if I do not, the Judge will hold me in contempt,* Mother Pig thought. She looked sadly at her once-little pigs with tears in her eyes and prepared to answer Counsel Boar's questions.

"Mother Pig, thanks for coming," said Counsel Boar. "I know this is hard for you, but can you tell us a little about your daughters when they were younger?"

Mother Pig wiped her eyes with her handkerchief, and between sniffles, she recounted her story.

"My daughters lied constantly when they were children. They never followed instructions, and my house was like a war zone. The constant bickering and contentious confrontations almost drove me crazy. Things got so bad that I even had a nervous breakdown, so I had to do the unthinkable; I put them out of my house. They had to fend for themselves. Can you imagine my suffering over the years knowing my three little piglets had to be on their own? Though they lived on their own, I still visited them and provided their necessities. I told them not to build straw houses or stick houses in the valley because the weather conditions continued to get worse each year, but only my eldest listened and built a brick house that withstood the tornado on that dreadful day."

"So, Mother Pig, is it your testimony that a tornado destroyed your daughters' houses and not Mr. Wolf?"

"Yes sir, it is. I knew all along that their story was implausible. There were even rumors to support my suspicions, but out of embarrassment, I kept quiet. What could I do? Nothing! They were grown, and they believed they knew it all."

Straw House Pig's face twisted into a grimace, and she made a rather loud gasp and clapped her right front hoof over her mouth. Her two sisters sheepishly bowed their heads and made no comments. Mother Pig looked directly at her three no-longer-little pigs and said tearfully, "I am sorry, girls, I cannot tell a lie, and I am under oath."

Counsel Boar, with a smile on his face said, "No further questions," satisfied with her answers.

On cross-examination, Ms. Priggly tried to impeach Mother Pig's testimony.

"So, Mother Pig, isn't it correct that the reason you threw your three defenseless daughters out of your house to fend for themselves was because you had remarried, and your new husband, Piggy Joe, did not want to be responsible for the care and feeding of three rapidly growing piglets?"

"THAT IS NOT TRUE; THE GIRLS WERE VERY DISOBEDIENT," Mother Pig shouted as tears streamed down her face.

"So you would like us to believe that your new husband and the three piglets got along splendidly with no hint of trouble in your domestic paradise?" Ms. Priggly asked. Mother Pig did not answer as she sobbed into a tissue hastily given to her by the court officer. She was dismayed anyone would even consider her a bad mother. Ms. Priggly did not wait for Mother Pig to answer; she just strutted to her seat and said, "No further questions." The courtroom was deadly quiet as Mother Pig continued to sob quietly into her now-soaked tissue.

Straw House Pig rushed to the front of the courtroom, ready to confront her mother and ask her the one question she had been dying to ask all her life. Today she was dressed in a checkered pink and white suit that sucked in her body bulges. She sported white pumps that barely fit her wide size-twelve feet and made loud tapping sounds as she walked.

"Mother Pig, which one of your three pigs do you love the most?" Straw House Pig asked. The courtroom grew decidedly quiet as many wondered about the relevancy of the question to the trial of Mr. Wolf. Mother Pig narrowed her eyes and looked at her daughter as she continued to dab her eyes.

"JUDGE, PLEASE COMMAND THIS WITNESS TO ANSWER THE QUESTION," yelled Straw House Pig. She dared not look at the Judge as she issued this directive.

"And the point of this question is?" the Judge asked as he looked at Straw House Pig intently.

"You will see," said Straw House Pig, "if you direct this witness to answer the question."

Many of the spectators in the court stifled their laughter as they watched the dark cloud that threatened to turn into a tsunami enveloping the Judge's face as he looked at Straw House Pig.

"I need to hear the relevancy now and not later, Ms. Straw House Pig," the Judge roared. Straw House Pig deflated like a balloon, as she had no answer for the Judge.

"Ms. Straw House Pig, sit down," ordered Judge Hognott. Straw House Pig walked meekly to her seat, and Mother Pig tearfully exited the witness box.

Later that evening, Mother Pig did an interview on Fox News to tell her side of the story. Many of the pigs were angry with her for testifying against her daughters.

"Tell us why you are here this evening, Mother Pig," the news anchor said.

"Well, I was subpoenaed by the defense to testify against my adorable piglets. You see how beautiful they are, and I just love them so much, but the subpoena clearly stated that if I did not comply, I would be in contempt of court and face jail time. I did not want to go to jail, so I obeyed the law. Once on the witness stand, I had to tell the truth because I had taken an oath to tell the truth and nothing but the truth; furthermore, my morals would not allow me to lie."

Mother Pig broke down in tears.

"This is the worst day of my life. I had to endure the hateful stares of the pigs in the courtroom and the verbal abuse they leveled at me on my way home. Now I fear for my life because I have received several death threats. They pester me on the phone, write hateful slogans on my walls, and on that thing they call imterret."

"Oh, you mean the internet," said the anchor, smiling sheepishly.

"Mother Pig, you have my sympathy," the anchor replied in a comforting voice. "You have to understand that pigs are good at intimidation. They have clearly resorted to bullying. It is their tactic to scare off a dear old pig doing her civic duty and following the law. This orchestrated campaign by the pigs to scare Mother Pig will not work if good citizens in the community stand by her."

It's was a mistake coming here, said Mother Pig to herself. Why is the news anchor saying these things? He is making an already bad situation worse.

Mother Pig hastily hurried out of the guest seat, more worried than ever about everyone's reaction to her testimony against her daughters, especially after her appearance on Fox News. She slowly walked home, hoping to avoid her tormentors. While she did not see anyone she knew, Mother Pig did not miss the contemptuous stares directed her way by some of the pigs eating at an outdoor café and the sneers of a pack of dogs standing idly at the corner shops.

Meanwhile over at MSNBC, Rachael Meadow mocked Mother Pig's testimony.

"Oh the love of a mother!" she exclaimed sarcastically. "That performance is worthy of an Oscar. I bet Mother Pig's lawyer coached her through many crying spells for her to get that good. Boo! Hoo! Hoo! I love my daughters sooo much that I could even testify against them. It seems Mother Pig's conscience got the better of her."

Rachael Meadow continued to imitate Mother Pig's emotional outburst on the witness stand. Her guest commentator that night laughed at Meadow's comments, and chimed in,

"Mother Pig basically threw her girls under the bus, plain and simple. I guess it's hard out there for a pig," continued the guest commentator as he and Rachael Meadow laughed hysterically.

CHAPTER TWENTY-NINE

ARE THEY BUSH PIGS?

That same night, CNN's Wolf Blitzer had Ms. Foxology, the anthropologist, on his program. Ms. Foxology was dressed in grey cargo pants with a white and green T-shirt that read "Save the World from Destruction." She wore grey socks with green and white high-top sneakers with words such as *environment, green, peace, vegetarian*, and *war* inscribed in various shades of red, green, and yellow. Her wild brown hair no longer confined by a barrette stuck out untidily in all directions. She peered through green square-framed glasses at Wolf Blitzer, who asked her about parent-child relationships as they related to the bush pig. Ms. Foxology energetically explained,

"Bush pigs are often driven off by their parents when they are very young, as in the case of The Three Little Pigs and Mother Pig. The bush pig is very aggressive and can be very wild, and this behavior is difficult to control. The culture of the bush pig puts them at odds with the rest of society."

Countless tweets and e-mails from many disgruntled bush pigs poured into CNN. "Our reputations are being besmirched." "That anthropologist is a farce; check out her credentials," some read. Angry pigs bombarded the corporate offices of CNN with threats. The pigs demanded the firing of Wolf Blitzer for allowing these bigoted remarks against the bush pig community. One bush pig e-mailed, "Warn that stupid big-haired fox masquerading as a professional to talk sense or else!" CNN officials said that they would review the matter as they watched their ratings increase, but their advertising dollars decrease.

Later in the program, Wolf Blitzer featured Mrs. Headfox, an accomplished psychologist with many letters behind her name such as PHD, MD, and MSW.

"Welcome to the program, Mrs. Headfox," he said. "Please shed some light on the controversy that surrounds the bush pig in today's society."

"Thank you for having me, Mr. Blitzer; it is my pleasure to be here," she replied.

"Studies have shown that bush pigs often feel trapped by how they are perceived in their communities, so they often rebel and fail to obey the norms of society. Furthermore, the adult bush pigs push their young out of the pen at an early age, so the young bush pigs often do not fully develop into mature rational beings. It is therefore not difficult to understand how The Three Pigs could have caused their mother so much trouble that she had to throw them out of the house at such a young age."

Brick House Pig, who was watching the program with her husband, immediately switched off the television.

"Imagine the insult," she fumed. "How dare this pompous idiot call me a bush pig?"

CHAPTER THIRTY

ARE YOU AN EXPERT?

The next day, Counsel Boar called Migs, the builder, to the stand. "Mr. Migs, how likely is it that a straw house could be blown down by a puff or a huff from a lone wolf?" asked Counsel Boar in an amused voice.

"Impossible," said Mr. Migs.

"What do you mean by impossible?" Counsel Boar asked.

"Well, you would need hundreds of wolves to demolish even a straw house," said Mr. Migs, laughing hysterically, clearly enjoying himself as he faced dozens of angry pigs who seemed ready to tear him to shreds.

"On what basis do you offer this opinion?" asked Counsel Boar.

"Well," Mr. Migs said in a defiant tone, "I come from a long line of builders, and I have not met a lone wolf capable of blowing down even a straw house, and I doubt I ever will."

"Now, Mr. Migs, would a stick house be able to stand up to a tornado?"

"No it would not."

"What about a straw house?"

"Definitely not."

"What about a brick house?"

"Yes, a brick house should be able to withstand a tornado."

"So Mr. Migs, would you give us your expert opinion about the most likely scenario that led to the destruction of the straw and stick houses? Could you say it was the huffing and puffing of a lone wolf or the force of a tornado going hundreds of miles a second?" asked Counsel Boar, clearly enjoying himself.

"I would definitively say it was the tornado that blew that straw house and stick house down."

"Why are you so sure, Mr. Migs?"

"Well, there is my experience plus an article dated July seventh that was published in the *Times,* a reputable newspaper, titled 'Lessons of a Glass House.'"

"Mr. Migs, can you tell us what this article is about?"

"It is about a straw house that was blown down because of wind," said Mr. Migs.

"You don't say," said Counsel Boar, feigning surprise.

"Yes, it explains right here that the straw house gave in when the wind blew," Mr. Migs said excitedly as he pointed to the article in the *Times* for Counsel Boar to see. Counsel Boar looked at the Judge and stated, "I ask your permission, please, for this article to be entered into evidence." The Judge nodded his assent to Counsel Boar, who handed a copy to the Bailiff, who handed the copy to the Judge.

"So would you say it was the strong winds from the tornado and not Mr. Wolf, as the pigs have claimed, that blew the straw house down?" asked Counsel Boar as if he already knew the answer.

"It would be ridiculous to believe that Mr. Wolf would have the strength to blow two houses down one behind the other; that is not logical," Mr. Migs said loudly.

"No further questions," said Counsel Boar as he walked back to his seat and started writing furiously.

Ms. Priggly sauntered to the front of the courtroom and circled the witness stand as if about to attack a prey. She seemed to be calculating her next move as she smoothed out her magnificent pinstriped blue and white three-piece pantsuit with a bead of pearls around her neck. Her wrist sparkled with a Bertolucci fascino eighteen-karat gold diamond watch. Ms. Priggly's blue-black hair swept back in a dramatic French chignon stood in stark contrast to her lips painted a frosty pink color. Her sheer stocking feet were set in a pair of black leather and snake skin high-heeled Prada. Despite the stuffiness of the courtroom, the spectators watched intently as Ms. Priggly strolled to the front in her usual trot-like fashion, never missing a step as she slowly pivoted around to face her audience after reaching the witness box. She slowly gulped down a glass of water, draining the glass to its last refreshing drop, before placing it on the witness box. Counsel Boar watched in hopeless fascination, knowing that things were about to get ugly.

Ms. Priggly did her customary slow eye scan around the courtroom as if to ensure she had everyone's attention. She settled her gaze on Mr. Migs, who squirmed quite uncomfortably in his seat. She fixated a long penetrating stare on Mr. Migs before saying in her rich British accent, "So Mr. Migs, did you ever see the straw house and the stick house in question?"

"No ma'am, I can't say I have," said Mr. Migs, getting more uncomfortable as Ms. Priggly continued to stare unblinkingly at him.

"So on what basis are you giving this so-called expert opinion?" Ms. Priggly asked Mr. Migs sarcastically.

"Well, as a builder," said Mr. Migs haughtily.

"So how many houses have you built, Mr. Migs—thirty, twenty, nine, eight, five, one?" Ms. Priggly let her voice trail off. She turned her back on Mr. Migs as if his answer was not important to her while staring at the faces of the jurors and the spectators in the courtroom. Mr. Migs seemed to turn a bright shade of red. "Mr. Migs, I can't hear you," said Ms. Priggly quite loudly as she walked toward the jurors, clearly enjoying putting Mr. Migs in the hot seat.

"I haven't actually built a house," said Mr. Migs haltingly, wishing he was anywhere but on this witness stand.

"But you offered yourself as an expert builder, Mr. Migs," said Ms. Priggly in an incredulous voice. "Mr. Migs, do you know that according to the dictionary, a builder would be defined as someone who has built something? So Mr. Migs, what have you built?"

Snickering and grunts floated around the courtroom as Ms. Priggly fired question after question at Mr. Migs. The Judge had to pound his gavel to quiet the noise level in the courtroom. Spectators in the courtroom felt as if Ms. Priggly was a champion boxer delivering blow after blow to Mr. Migs' testimony, but more so to his pride. It was clear the pigs in the courtroom were enjoying this spectacular performance. One middle-aged pig muttered under her breath,

"That's a serious reality check for that proud fool."

The pigs beamed proudly because Ms. Priggly lived up to her reputation as a barracuda in a skirt. For the first time, the pigs felt as if they could win their case. The wolves, on the other hand, were fuming, since they felt Counsel Boar should do something and fast. The onslaught of questions Ms. Priggly leveled at Mr. Migs made some of the wolves gasp in disbelief.

Why wasn't Counsel Boar, that dumb pig, raising any objections? They wondered. Some of the wolves cast icy glares at the back of Counsel Boar's head, and some felt Mr. Wolf had been silly to hire a pig to represent him. One young wolf decided to help Counsel Boar out and yelled,

"OBJECTIONS, YOUR HONOR! MS. PRIGGLY IS BADGERING THE WITNESS."

This wolf had heard this phrase many times during the many hours he spent watching reruns of *Law and Order*. Clearly frustrated with Counsel Boar, he forgot he was not the plaintiff's lawyer. The courtroom became deathly still as the objection rang through the air. Judge Hognott, Ms. Priggly, Counsel Boar, the jury, and the courtroom spectators stared in fascination at the wolf before Judge Hognott bellowed,

"REMOVE THIS LAWYER WANNABE FROM THIS COURTROOM FORTHWITH! HE IS NOT AN ATTORNEY, THUS HE SHOULD KEEP HIS BIG FAT MOUTH SHUT AND LET COUNSEL BOAR DO OR NOT DO HIS JOB."

The pigs in the courtroom laughed at this comment as they waited impatiently for Ms. Priggly to continue making mincemeat of Mr. Migs.

After Judge Hognott got the courtroom under control, he ordered Ms. Priggly to continue her cross-examination. Ms. Priggly smiled and said, "My pleasure, Your Honor! So you were saying, Mr. Migs, before we were so rudely interrupted, that you have not built one solitary thing." Ms. Priggly clearly enjoyed emphasizing this point.

"I didn't say I was a builder; I said I come from a long line of builders," squeaked Mr. Migs.

"Oh, really, Mr. Migs, but you described yourself as an expert. You are aware that coming from a family of builders does not make one a builder, just like coming from a long line of doctors does not make one a doctor."

Counsel Boar yelled, "Objection!"

Some of the wolves sighed to themselves and thought, "*It seems that darn pig, Counsel Boar, had finally woken up from his slumber.*"

"On what grounds?" The Judge asked quietly.

"Ms. Priggly is badgering the witness," said Counsel Boar.

"I do not believe she is," said the Judge in a relatively calm voice. "Objection overruled. You may continue your line of questioning, Ms. Priggly."

"No further questions, Your Honor," replied Ms. Priggly triumphantly.

Shocked and surprised, Mr. Migs hurried off the witness stand and out of the courtroom to distance himself from the obvious hostility of the pigs in the courtroom. This concluded the testimony for that day.

CHAPTER THIRTY-ONE

MEDIA OUT-TAKE

On CNN that night, news commentators discussed the trial. One news anchor said that Ms. Priggly had roasted Mr. Migs alive. Another commentator asked in an incredulous manner, "Why Counsel Boar would put such an idiot on the witness stand to testify?"

"Mr. Migs's testimony is important," replied Wolf Blitzer, "because he presents a good case for his client as it relates to the plausibility of Mr. Wolf's ability to blow down the two pigs' houses."

Some of the commentators reluctantly agreed. The commentators animatedly discussed the legal strategies of Counsel Boar and Ms. Priggly for the remainder of the news segment.

On ESPN, one sports commentator compared the trial to a boxing match between Ms. Priggly, a heavyweight boxer, and a lightweight adversary, Counsel Boar.

"Don't count out Counsel Boar just yet," one analyst argued. "He might look quiet and unassuming—a bit like the underdog, but his strategy is brilliant, since he is building a solid case against a firmly entrenched myth of the wolf blowing down the two pigs' homes."

On Fox News, Mr. Sanity had Russell as his guest. Russell was the wolf who had shouted out an objection in the courtroom. The Fox News commentator proudly congratulated him on such a risky move in contrast to the cowardice of Counsel Boar. Russell was school-aged and very bright. He had played hooky from school that day just to watch the trial. He laughed and replied,

"Mr. Wolf is my hero; he is challenging the status quo despite incredible odds. What we are dealing with is simply a story concocted by three lying pigs that has evolved into a myth. The public never questioned the myth's validity, and it has harmed the wolf community for decades. As a result, it has always been difficult for wolves to have a bright future, particularly in a legal community controlled by pigs. As a result, many wolves have been forced to open their own businesses just to survive."

"Brilliantly articulated," replied Anchor Sanity.

"I belong to the community of wolves, Mr. Sanity, so I know firsthand the daily injustice meted out to us. When I sat in that courtroom, I felt it was my civic duty as a wolf to stand in solidarity with Mr. Wolf against those bald-faced liars. It was with honor that I was tossed out of the courtroom, even though I later faced the wrath of my parents and the headmistress at my school, and some of the parents who are not too pleased with me either."

Russell looked directly into the camera and said, "I would do it again without question because a wolf has to do what a wolf has to do. It's the only honorable recourse under the circumstances."

"There you have it, ladies and gentlemen; the young shall lead in this fight against systematic injustice," said Mr. Sanity.

He urged his viewers to call the headmistress and Russell's parents and implore them to treat him as a hero rather than to punish him.

"It's imperative that wolves and foxes turn out every day in great numbers and pack that courtroom in support of Mr. Wolf in his time of need," Mr. Sanity said.

"Be brave! Be counted! Be a winner! Be proactive!" he admonished his audience while pounding the desk with his fist.

CHAPTER THIRTY-TWO

WAS THE MOTIVE INSURANCE?

The following day, Counsel Boar called Mr. Actuary, an insurance expert, to the stand. He was to testify as to whether his company had insured the homes of The Three Pigs. Mr. Actuary was a bone-thin man. He was suntanned and all suited up in a Giorgio Armani grey herringbone striped two-piece suit with flat front trousers and a long-sleeved grey button-down shirt. A red Ricco tie with Savatore Ferragamo clay loafers, red binders, and a pocket calculator complemented his attire. He seemed ill at ease as if he would have been more comfortable in a corporate office than in a stuffy old courtroom..

"Mr. Actuary was there a policy on the home of Straw House Pig?" asked Counsel Boar.

"No, according to my records, I would not say there was a policy," Mr. Actuary said as he perused his notes.

"And why wasn't there a policy, Mr. Actuary?"

"Our insurance company, P.I.G, thought it was too risky to insure a house made of straw," said Mr. Actuary.

"You don't say," said Counsel Boar in an incredulous voice. "Do you know of any other insurance company that would have insured the straw house?"

"Objection Your Honor!" yelled Ms. Priggly."

"On what grounds?"

"Counsel Boar's question calls for conjecture on the part of Mr. Actuary unless he can tell us the basis of his knowledge of what other companies did or did not do as it relates to the insuring of Straw Pig's house," said Ms. Priggly in a sharp tone.

"Mr. Actuary, do you have firsthand knowledge of any other specific insurance company decisions on straw houses?" asked Judge Hognott.

"Yes, I do," Mr. Actuary answered.

"Objection overruled," Judge Hognott said. Ms. Priggly fumed and looked at Counsel Boar with utter disdain. "You may proceed with your questions, Counsel Boar," Judge Hognott said.

"Do you know of any other insurance company that would have insured the straw house?" Counsel Boar asked again

"No I do not," said Mr. Actuary

Counsel Boar asked Mr. Actuary, "What would you say were the risks of insuring that straw house?"

"Very risky," said Mr. Actuary.

"Now on a scale of one to ten, with one being the most risky and ten the least risky, where would you place the risk of a straw house? Remember, base your answer on a scale of one to ten," said Counsel Boar as he surveyed the jurors in the courtroom to see how well they were following this line of questioning. Two of the pig jurors appeared to be sleeping, one even slightly snoring, while the rest of the jurors seemed to be looking intently at Mr. Actuary.

"The straw house was a very high risk so I would say one," said Mr. Actuary. An audible gasp among the many canines resonated throughout the courtroom. The wolves nodded their heads in agreement and smiled. They were pleased with this response.

"Now, Mr. Actuary was there an insurance policy on the stick house?" asked Counsel Boar.

"Yes, there was," said Mr. Actuary.

"Why?"

"The risk was not as great on the stick house property as opposed to the straw house."

"On a scale of one to ten, how would you rate the stick house?"

"I would say a five in terms of risk."

"And your company was willing to take that risk, Mr. Actuary?"

"Yes, it was, considering the payout from the policy was really small."

"Did you insure Brick House Pig?"

"Yes, we did," said Mr. Actuary, "Since that house was really strong."

"Why would you say this particular brick house was so strong?"

"It was quite strong because it was made of brick and mortar, which are the materials approved by the housing authority for the construction of houses," said Mr. Actuary, as if it was self-explanatory.

"Now, Mr. Actuary, have you ever insured a straw house?"

"Never," said Mr. Actuary. "Emphatically no."

"And why not?" asked Counsel Boar, moving closer to Mr. Actuary as if they were about to share a secret and Counsel Boar could not wait to hear the answer.

"Well, it would not make good business sense to insure a structure as weak as a straw house," said Mr. Actuary with obvious impatience.

"Now, Mr. Actuary, does your insurance company, P.I.G cover natural disasters?" Counsel Boar asked Mr. Actuary as he looked at the jurors.

"No, we do not. Many other companies have similar policies."

"Did your company cover damages by wolves?

"Yes it did."

"No further questions," said Counsel Boar as he walked back to his seat.

Ms. Priggly began her cross-examination of Mr. Actuary in her usual dramatic fashion. Today she was wearing a stunning sky-blue designer two-piece suit. Some media outlets would later speculate that it was a designer original from Oscar de la Renta and estimated to cost thousands of dollars. She was wearing her customary high-heeled shoes, but today the shoes were a startling royal blue in color. Her unusually thick hair tied back in its customary bun gave her a no-nonsense appearance. The scarlet lipstick that lined her rather full wide lips was a lovely contrast to her sleek attire. Many of the female spectators looked on with envy and admiration, since Ms. Priggly's courtroom wardrobe was one of the highlights of the trial. Even some of the male wolves and foxes grudgingly admitted to themselves that Ms. Priggly was one good-looking pig, whose luscious lips were very appealing, especially in lipstick.

"Mr. Actuary isn't it correct that insurance companies are notorious for not wanting to pay out claims?" Ms. Priggly asked this question in her usual in-your-face style. The momentary fixation with her appearance immediately shifted back to her line of questioning.

Mr. Actuary was squirming in his seat uncomfortably. Others in his firm who had the misfortune of being on the opposing side of Ms. Priggly had warned him about her. Beads of sweat popped out on forehead as he stuttered, "That is not correct."

"Can you please tell us how much money your company, P.I.G, paid out last year in claims?" Ms. Priggly asked. Mr. Actuary pulled out his pocket calculator and attempted to tap in some numbers.

"Let me make this simple," said Ms. Priggly before he could give an answer. "Did your company, P.I.G, pay out more money in claims than it denied in claims?" She was clearly enjoying the discomfort evident on Mr. Actuary's face. He seemed hesitant to answer the question and appeared to turn various shades of red. Ms. Priggly produced a white sheet of paper from her folder and asked Judge Hognott in an ever-so-sweet voice,

"May I have your permission to approach the bench?" Judge Hognott nodded his assent, and Ms. Priggly approached the Judge in her usual trot-like fashion. She handed Judge Hognott the paper after asking his permission to offer it as an exhibit. Judge Hognott nodded yes.

CHAPTER THIRTY-TWO

"Your Honor and members of the jury, I would like to offer this as exhibit C—documents specifying P.I.G's claim record." Ms. Priggly sauntered back to the witness stand and fixed her stare on Mr. Actuary.

"So, Mr. Actuary, have you been able to recollect whether your company, P.I.G, denied more claims than they approved?"

At this point, Mr. Actuary appeared to recover his voice and weakly squeaked,

"P.I.G denied more claims than they paid out, but only because …"

He was cut off promptly by Ms. Priggly, who yelled,

"NO FURTHER QUESTIONS," as she sashayed to her seat, quite satisfied with the way her cross-examination of Mr. Actuary had turned out. As she took her seat, Ms. Priggly looked over at her niece, Ms. Sow, and whispered,

"Learn from the best." Ms. Sow smiled approvingly. She was proud of her aunt's overall performance throughout the case, and she hoped that one day she would be half as good an attorney as Auntie Priggly.

CHAPTER THIRTY-THREE

TEACHER DEAREST

The next day Counsel Boar called Ida White to the witness stand. Straw House Pig let out a loud gasp when she saw Ida White. Now she was upset she had neglected to look at the witness list. The opposing attorneys had handed her the list with tons of other court documents. Straw House Pig wondered how it was possible that that old witch was still alive. She had to be at least a century by now.

Ida White, a painfully thin pig, hobbled to the stand. Safety pins held in place her knee-high stockings. The stockings looked quite wrinkled until you realized you were seeing her badly wrinkled skin showing through her sheer stockings. Her thin legs seemed incapable of getting her to her destination, so her walker aided in the process. Two wooden sticks held her shockingly white hair in a tight bun affixed to the back of her head. As she slowly sat down in the witness box, Ms. Ida White bemoaned the pain in her back caused by the long bus ride from sunny Florida where she now lived. She had to ride the Greyhound Bus into

Maplewood because she refused to set foot on a plane. Ms. White was quite happy when Counsel Boar had asked her to testify. Coming to Maplewood broke the monotony of playing bingo everyday and listening to her best friend, dear old Agnes. Agnes was a chronic complainer and constantly whined about her aches and pain, and about the fact that her children hated to talk to her. Ida suspected that the children hardly called Agnes because she complained so much and was always creating confusion amongst her children. Ida was also most delighted to be back in Maplewood to catch up with old friends who had not yet drawn their last breath.

Most of the occupants in the courtroom eagerly awaited the identity of the witness who had gotten Straw House Pig so rattled. They scrutinized the figure now seated in the box, seemingly eager to begin her testimony. Ms. Ida White's eyes danced with merriment, belying her advanced age as she watched with fascination how all eyes in the courtroom centered on her. She wished her students had been this attentive when she had been teaching English before she had retired.

Counsel Boar smiled quite broadly as he looked at Ms. Ida White and asked, "Ms. Ida White, do you know any of the parties in this case?"

"Oh yes, I do," said Ms. White quite cheerfully as she peered at the front row on the right hand side of the courtroom, coming eye to eye with Straw House Pig, who was openly fuming and glaring at her.

"Why is this old biddy sitting here alive in this courtroom back here in Maplewood; shouldn't she be dead by now?" she muttered angrily under her breath.

"And who would that be?" continued Counsel Boar as he took off his glasses, cleaned the lenses with his handkerchief, and then placed them back on his face.

"Straw House Pig," Ms. White said quite excitedly as if she were a contestant on a game show.

"And in what capacity did you know her?"

Mr. Wolf was sitting to the left of Straw House Pig on the opposite side of the aisle. He sat up with great expectation when he saw the effect this little old sow in the floral light-blue polyester blouse, blue skirt, laced-up brown shoes, and no-nonsense attitude was having on Straw House Pig. Evidently, Straw House Pig was terrified of what this witness had to say, because she was fanning herself frantically as if her life depended on it.

"Well, I was her eighth grade teacher," Ms White answered as she wiped her clammy hoofs on her skirt.

"Now what kind of student would you say Straw House Pig was?" asked Counsel Boar as he leaned on the witness box and watched Straw House Pig and the jury simultaneously.

"Oh dear, she was quite mischievous. She never paid attention in class, never finished her work, and at recess she was just the worst, always pelting other students with rocks or her lunch."

Ms. Ida never took her eyes off Straw House Pig as she remembered the pranks Straw House Pig had even played on her.

At that moment, Straw House Pig could not decide whom she hated more. Did she hate Mr. Wolf or this old biddy, Ms. White? Why didn't they both die of old age? She wondered miserably as she sweated like a roasted pig at a barbeque. Right now all Straw House Pig was painfully aware of was that she was being carved up and literally thrown to the wolves. Whoever said teachers were supposed to be caring, Straw House Pig wondered as she wished for the umpteenth time that Ms. Ida White and Mr. Wolf would just drop dead. As Ms. Ida White testified, Straw House Pig noticed that her two sisters stared painfully ahead, both contorting their faces as Ms. White gleefully recounted some of Straw House Pig's antics in and out the classroom. Ms. White even had the nerve to have her old grade books as she read out Straw House Pig's big fat Fs along with her comments on grade reports: "Failure to follow directions," "Unable to sit still," "Not likely to amount to much." She continued her testimony by further stating that Straw House Pig constantly stole from the other students, pelted them with food in the lunchroom, and exhibited aggressive and unruly behavior constantly. "Many of the other pigs even referred to Straw House Pig as a bush pig," said Ms. White as she stared at Straw House Pig with obvious contempt.

"ENOUGH, YOU OLD CRONE!" Straw House Pig shrieked loudly as she bolted to the witness stand, ready to decimate Ms. White. The court officer grabbed Straw House Pig just in the nick of time as she was about to whack Ms. White across her face with her right front hoof. Ms. White ducked under the desk in the witness stand, holding up her hands to shield her face.

She shrieked in fright,

"Oh dear! Oh dear! This is most dreadful! I'm being attacked." Ms. White looked visibly shaken. Consequently, Counsel Boar helped her back into her chair.

"It's all right, Ms. White. You are safe; no one is going to hurt you."

"I am not so sure of that," Ms. White replied, eyeing Straw House Pig nervously.

"I can see that this pig has not changed one bit," she continued as she nervously tried to smooth the folds of her skirt. Straw House Pig's sisters shook their heads in dismay, and looked at Straw House Pig angrily. The courthouse audience erupted in shock as Judge Hognott banged his gavel repeatedly and threatened to charge Straw House Pig with contempt of court.

Mr. Wolf smirked and put his head in his lap. Things seem to be shaping up rather nicely, he thought. Ms. Priggly wished again that she had secured separate trials for The Three Pigs. *This darn Straw House Pig was definitely more trouble than she was worth*, Ms. Priggly thought as she furiously wrote on her yellow legal pad.

CHAPTER THIRTY-FOUR

PLAINTIFF'S CASE IN CHIEF: THE THREE PIGS TELL THEIR STORY

For the defense, the pigs' attorney, Ms. Priggly, called The Three Little Pigs to testify. They each told the same old story that the wolf had blown the two pigs' houses down and had attempted unsuccessfully to blow the third pig's brick house down. Stick House Pig even feigned fear of Mr. Wolf, and cried pitifully as Ms. Priggly questioned her.

"I am still scared of that wicked old wolf," she moaned while wiping tears from her eyes. "I find it hard to be under the same roof with him. Since his attack, my life has never been the same again."

Counsel Boar called Brick House Pig to the witness stand for cross-examination, Counsel Boar asked, "Did you or didn't you write a story about Mr. Wolf blowing your sisters' houses down and trying to kill you?"

"Yes," said Brick House Pig.

"Did you publish this book?"

"Yes I did."

"No further questions," said Counsel Boar, smiling.

On cross-examination, Counsel Boar tried to impeach the credibility of Straw House Pig. He asked Straw House Pig as she sat on the witness stand, "Can you please tell us what the weather was like on the day you said Mr. Wolf came to your house?"

Straw House Pig was dressed in a satiny white jumpsuit that gave her the appearance of a boiled egg. Two of the buttons from the pantsuit had already hit the floor after losing their ability to reach the buttonholes due to Straw House Pig's excessive weight. Straw House Pig sat squirming uncomfortably in the witness stand and muttered,

"I do not recall; it was a really long time ago."

Counsel Boar asked, "You expect us to believe that you do not recall the weather conditions on the day you just described as the worst day of your life?"

Straw House Pig remained silent.

"Are you disputing the testimony of Mr. Whistle Pig, who keeps accurate records for the Bureau of Weather and has been employed in that capacity for several decades?"

Straw House Pig replied angrily, "I said I do not remember." She began to scratch herself intensely, and one reporter whispered to himself, "Unbelievable. Is she breaking out in hives or something?" as he trained the cameras on her.

"Objection!" shouted Ms. Priggly.

"On what grounds?" asked the Judge peering over his half–glasses, seeming to forget momentarily that Ms. Priggly was not Straw House Pig's attorney.

"Counsel Boar is badgering the witness," replied Ms. Priggly loudly while peering at the Judge and scanning the room as if to get the jury and the other pigs involved in this intense courtroom drama.

"YOUR HONOR, WHY IS SHE OBJECTING? SHE IS NOT EVEN STRAW HOUSE PIG'S ATTORNEY," yelled Counsel Boar, furious at this turn of events. Counsel Boar felt the Judge was letting Ms. Priggly get away with ignoring the court's rules.

Judge Hognott paused and looked at both the attorneys, then addressed Counsel Boar. "Are you badgering the witness?"

"I am not," said Counsel Boar angrily. "I am just trying to get this lying pig to tell the truth and nothing but the truth, Your Honor."

"Watch your mouth, Counsel Boar, before I find you in contempt of court," said the Judge quietly before turning to Ms. Priggly. "Sorry, but I will have to overrule you on this because I just want to get to the truth of the matter—this case has gone on long enough."

"WHAT A FARCE OF A TRIAL," yelled one of the pigs in the audience.

Again, the Judge slammed down his gavel and ordered the Bailiff to escort the yelling pig from the courtroom. Everyone in the courtroom became silent. No one wanted the Judge to toss him out on his or her ears like that pig. The other pigs in the courtroom waited with baited breaths for Counsel Boar's next question.

"Was it plausible and extremely likely that based on the weather conditions on the day in question, Mr. Wolf had just been looking for shelter from the tornado?"

Why is this old ugly pig using such big words, Straw House Pig wondered. Plausible, extremely likely. What the heck does this traitor pig mean? Straw House Pig's head bubbled over with possibilities.

"Could you repeat the question?" asked Straw House Pig after a long pause. She needed to buy herself some time to get her thoughts together before answering the question.

"Was it plausible and extremely likely that based on the weather conditions on the day in question, Mr. Wolf had just been looking for shelter from the tornado?" asked Counsel Boar again.

Straw House Pig felt like she was a contestant on a game show who needed to guess herself right into the correct answer. Realizing she still did not quite know what Counsel Boar was asking, she took a deep breath, swallowed her pride, and asked in a small voice,

"Counsel Boar, could you please rephrase the question so that I can understand what you are asking?"

Counsel Boar smiled as comprehension dawned.

"Straw House Pig is it possible that Mr. Wolf was simply looking for shelter from the elements on the day in question?" asked Counsel Boar as if he were talking to a child.

"NO," yelled Straw House Pig, quite frustrated.

"So, while you claim you cannot remember the big dangerous tornado that caused damage to straw homes in the area where you lived, you still expect us to believe that you remember the reason Mr. Wolf came knocking on your door on that day so long ago, as you stated in your previous answers?"

"Yes," said Straw House Pig defiantly.

"So you are absolutely one hundred percent certain that the wolf was knocking on your door to make a feast of you, just as you remember the weather on the day in question?"

"Yes…I mean no," stammered Straw House Pig, wishing she were anywhere but on the witness stand. She could not endure the glares of hundreds of pigs who seemed to be piercing holes through her with their eyes.

"Objection!" yelled Ms. Priggly.

"On what grounds?" The Judge stared at both attorneys as he asked this question.

"Counsel Boar is quite clearly confusing the witness," said Ms. Priggly angrily.

"Overruled," replied Judge Hognott. "Straw House Pig should raise that objection."

Straw House Pig appeared tired, defeated, and oblivious to the discussion. She remained silent, not sure what the Judge and Ms. Priggly were debating. She just wanted to get off the witness stand. The countless hostile stares of furious-looking wolves, foxes, and angry pigs frightened Straw House Pig. Ms. Priggly glared at both Counsel Boar and the Judge.

"No further questions," said Counsel Boar with a satisfied look on his face as he practically danced back to his seat.

Straw House Pig sobbed uncontrollably as the Bailiff escorted her off the witness stand. She just knew she had made a mess of her testimony, and this suspicion was confirmed when she sat down next to her sisters. The two pigs ignored her completely. They were clearly angry at Straw House Pig's performance on the witness stand, and she felt like the sacrificial pig. The only bright note in this whole matter was that if Mr. Wolf did win the case, he would get nothing. She was broke, and her piggy bank account was quite empty. Straw House Pig smiled in spite of herself.

At noon, the Judge called a recess and emphatically declared that closing arguments would start the following day.

"All rise," said the Bailiff as Judge Hognott left the courtroom.

"CLEAR THE COURTROOM," the Bailiff yelled when it appeared the spectators did not want to leave. Instead, they were whispering among themselves, speculating what would take place during the closing arguments. Others were discussing what they thought Ms. Priggly would wear to court, as they knew she would go out with a bang.

After several warnings and threats of arrest, everyone scurried out of the courtroom. The pigs were quite upset and huddled outside the court building complaining about the Judge's unfairness. The wolves, standing in packs near the courtroom steps, appeared happier than the pigs because they felt as if things were finally looking up for them.

The trial of *Mr. Wolf v. The Three Pigs* dominated all the news channels that night as each commentator for the respective sides argued that the truth was on their side. The news commentators on MSNBC argued that the pigs had done a great job sticking to their story. "Straw House Pig seems like the weakest link of the lot, and this might compromise the case," one commentator said thoughtfully.

Fox News commentators seemed gleeful, and one anchor gloated,

"I told you not to underestimate Counsel Boar. Did you see how he crucified Straw House Pig on the witness stand?" Another commentator asked,

"Did you see the big act that Stick House Pig put on the stand when questioned by Ms. Priggly? I do believe that Ms. Priggly coached her to act the part, but only a fool would buy into that pretentious sham she put on."

The blogosphere was going crazy as people posted their views of how the trial was going. Some argued that Counsel Boar had made Straw House Pig look like a fool. Others blamed Counsel Boar for the intimidating tactics he used against Straw House Pig in her most vulnerable moments. "Who wouldn't break down on the witness stand when confronted by that burly monster?" one pig wrote.

The following day was the last day of the trial. Spectators filled the courtroom. Some supporters came for the first time from all over the country, determined not to miss the final phase of such a momentous occasion. One wealthy furry white wolf had even flown in from Sweden to show his support for Mr. Wolf. For the first time since the trial, the canines outnumbered the pigs by almost two to one in the courtroom. The wolves appeared cheerful, believing that finally, their day in court had come and their vindication was inevitable.

CHAPTER THIRTY-FIVE

CLOSING ARGUMENTS

Ms. Priggly, dressed in Jimmy Choo red high heels and a Bashy red two-piece pantsuit, strutted to the front of the courtroom. Her heels made a tapping sound for each step she took. She looked around the courtroom, at the wolves, and then at the Jury for about two minutes before she proceeded to speak.

"Members of the jury, this case is simple; it is a case of truth versus fiction. Many of you have heard the truth as told by The Three Pigs and recorded in the history books. Now Counsel Boar and Mr. Wolf have spun a tall tale otherwise known as fiction that they would like us to believe so many years after the fact. The truth of the matter is that Mr. Wolf tried to harm The Three Little Pigs and was unsuccessful. Today the wolf sits before us in this courtroom masquerading as a wolf in sheep's clothing, hoping to trick you into believing he is harmless. Today he hopes to wear the role of the victim, poor Mr. Wolf. Mr. Wolf would like us to believe that these three little pigs tried to harm him." Ms. Priggly let out a high shrill laugh that appeared to pierce the silence in the court-room. "Mr. Wolf would like us to believe that he, the *'big bad wolf,'* was afraid of Three *little* Pigs." The pigs' attorney emphasized the word *little*.

"The *'big bad wolf'* claimed he was looking for shelter from the storm. Members of the jury, I know you are not gullible. The truth of the matter is as plain as day. Jurors, I do not want you to see Mr. Wolf as he appears now many years later, but imagine him as he was many years ago on the day he decided to stalk and then hunt down The Three Little Pigs. Imagine him without the cane, quite agile, and with the ability to sprint, not just run extremely fast. Mr. Wolf was a smooth talker, but those who knew him best will tell you that he was also dangerous. His teeth were sharper then, and his brain even more calculating than today. Mr. Wolf had a reputation around town as the wolf not to mess with. Many pigs in this courtroom can attest to his aggression and hostility toward them. His notoriety had preceded him even beyond the bound-aries of Maplewood, so when he encountered those three little pigs, it was not a friendly visit, and it was certainly not a cry for help."

"It is plain and simple that Mr. Wolf's only intention on the day in question was to harm the pigs. However, he was unable to, so he decided to make up a story to save his reputation. There is one undeniable truth, and that is that the *'big bad wolf'* huffed and puffed and blew down two little pigs' houses. They are all grown up now, but just imagine them as frail, defenseless teenagers devoid of parental protection back then. They barely escaped with their lives, but the wolf pursued them to the safety of the third little pig's house to eat them all up, and instead liter-ally found himself in hot water. The only reason these three pigs are here today to tell their story is because Mr. Wolf made a mistake and slipped. More importantly, these three little pigs, just like many other pigs that dangerous wolves try to prey on, never let their guards down. Members of the jury do not let your guard down, not even for a second. Do not believe this slimy old wolf. He is a liar, a stalker, and a predator. You know this. I know this. Moreover, the world knows this, so forget whatever Mr. Wolfs' attorney stated about the *'big bad wolf'* being scared on the day he blew these houses down. Do not believe it. It is just one big old fat lie!" stated Ms. Priggly looking directly at the plaintiff, Mr. Wolf, as she strutted to her seat.

The courtroom became still as the occupants digested Ms. Priggly's appeal to the jury to dismiss Mr. Wolf's case against the pigs. Some of the pigs sat nervously on the edge of their seats pondering what Counsel Boars' closing argument would be. A younger pig bowed her head prayerfully and made the sign of the cross, hoping for a miracle for the defendants.

A gruff old wolf sitting close to her smiled sheepishly and whispered, "Do not even try to pray. You are unclean, remember." The pig glared at him angrily and looked the other way.

All eyes focused on Counsel Boar, who waited a full five minutes after Ms. Priggly's speech before he started his closing arguments. Counsel Boar was dressed conservatively in a dark-blue Brooks Brothers suit with a dark-blue bow tie and shiny black sharkskin shoes. This was a stark contrast to his appearance on the first day of the trial. Some of the spectators thought he looked more like a lawyer today than the seedy car salesperson of the past weeks. Counsel Boar smiled broadly, as he approached the jurors of pigs and wolves. He trotted over to face the jurors and said, "Members of the jury have you ever told a white lie that got out of control?"

He paused for a minute, then said, "Well, members of the jury, this is a case about three pigs that started off with a little white lie that got out of control. The mother of The Three Pigs told them to erect strong houses. Their mother and the rest of the community told the pigs to use durable materials; however, two of the pigs did not follow instructions. As a result, the tornado blew their houses down. The two pigs did not adhere to the standard building requirements, considering that they lived in an area prone to floods and storms. These two pigs did not want to take responsibility for not building houses that were strong enough to withstand a tornado. Instead, they chose to blame an innocent wolf who happened to be in the neighborhood looking for shelter from the storm-- a wolf who only minutes earlier had tried to keep one of these pigs out of trouble. Instead of helping Mr. Wolf during a tornado by letting him into their houses, they chose to blame him for blowing down their houses in order to get the sympathy of the other pigs in their community rather than much deserved ridicule.

"Remember, members of the jury, the third little pig who listened to her mother and the community built her house with bricks. The tornado did not blow down her house. Unfortunately, the third pig chose to join her two little sisters in a lie. Furthermore, when Straw House Pig and Stick House Pig found out they would not collect any insurance proceeds due to a natural disaster, they had to blame someone. They chose Mr. Wolf, who happened to be at the wrong place at the wrong time. Consequently, The Three Pigs lied on Mr. Wolf to cover their hides. Then the pigs communicated these lies to others in the community, and these lies caused harm to Mr. Wolf's reputation, not just in his community but all around the world.

"Remember, this tornado was not a figment of Mr. Wolf's imagination. It did happen. We had a groundhog who testified to that. We had The Three Pigs' mother who testified that The Three Little Pigs gave her loads of trouble. As a result, she had to throw them out of her home. Imagine how bad The Three Little Pigs were for Mother Pig to throw all three out of the house to fend for themselves. Members of the jury, the facts are clear; the pigs blamed Mr. Wolf for something he did not do. They blamed Mr. Wolf for an act of nature, something that was out of his control, all because of a lie that sprang out of control. The Three Pigs told these lies because they were in need of an alibi to hide their shame.

"Members of the jury, the pigs' theory has been tried, tested, and proven false. Several years ago, Samson, a powerful wolf, younger and stronger than Mr. Wolf in his heyday, decided to prove he was stronger than Mr. Wolf was. Samson was confident, sure of himself, and very proud, so he built a house similar to Straw Pig's House. In front of several witnesses, pigs and wolves alike, he tried to blow the house down. Today Samson is a mere shadow of himself. He huffed and puffed so hard that all he experienced was a nervous breakdown. He has been to several doctors, and even they could not help him. Because of this silliness, he shakes constantly, finds it hard to concentrate, and speaks in a squeaky almost inaudible voice. Samson is present in this courtroom today, but he is so ashamed of his foolish behavior that he will not admit it in public. If a wolf twice the size and strength of Mr. Wolf could not blow one straw house down, how likely is it that a wounded Mr. Wolf could blow two houses down?"

"LIAR! YOU LIE!" shouted a burly red-faced pig that shot up from his seat to confront Counsel Boar.

"Remove this insolent miscreant from my presence forthwith," roared Judge Hognott, as he loudly slammed his gavel on the desk. Nelly Pig shrieked loudly in fright from the unexpected interruption. "I'm so tired of these bumbling idiots," muttered the Bailiff under his breath as he dragged the disruptive pig out of the courtroom. Counsel Boar seemed a little shaken by this unexpected outburst, but he cleared his throat, straightened his tie, and resumed his discourse.

"Members of the jury don't be fooled by these villains." He pointed to The Three Pigs. "They must be made to pay for their vicious attacks on Mr. Wolf's life and his reputation." Everyone in the courtroom looked at the wolves, wondering which one was Samson, but the wolves all sat stone-faced and focused their attention on Counsel Boar.

"These pigs harmed Mr. Wolf when Straw House Pig pelted him with apples. The Three Pigs injured Mr. Wolf when he fell in a big boiling pot of water and suffered third-degree burns. Since this is a civil trial, members of the jury, I want you to concentrate on how these three Pigs defamed Mr. Wolf by concocting a story that became the subject of a book, movies, and countless conversations. As a result, an innocent wolf and his progeny remain universally censured because they are wolves. Members of the jury, I want you to view the bigger picture. Look beyond today and light years into the future, even after we all cease to exist, and ask yourselves the question: 'How will this story affect the generations of wolves to come?'

"The damage done to this community has cataclysmic implications. Take into consideration that Mr. Wolf has to live on the outskirts of Maplewood just because he is a wolf. He is unable to enjoy the blessings of mainstream society the way we do because of the lies of three pigs who are living comfortably off the proceeds of their shameless false-hood. These three pigs have destroyed countless wolves' lives. Members of the jury, Mr. Wolf cannot help that he was born a wolf and considered a prey by those of you who read stories such as Little Red Riding Hood. You must judge this case based on the hard, cold facts rather than public opinion. The story concocted by The Three Pigs was a hoax. Members of the jury, I would like you to examine the evidence you heard in court the last couple of weeks and come to a just conclusion, and that is that Mr. Wolf, an honorable and upright citizen of Maplewood, deserves to have his name cleared and get his clean reputation back.

"Furthermore, The Three Lying pigs should pay for their lies by dipping into their piggy banks and repaying Mr. Wolf. They made millions off his pain and suffering. Large corporations made billions and are still profiting off publications of this story. Walk around your neighborhood stores, and count the many memorabilia manufactured in the name of the characters in this story. How many members of the audience sitting right here have purchased caricatures of Mr. Wolf? I ask again, how many T-shirts have you seen stamped with logos of The Three Little Pigs. The earning power of this saga has grown legs, wings, and wheels with far-reaching earning power globally. The story of The Three Little Pigs circulated in over a hundred languages has haunted the life of Mr. Wolf and his family. Do you know how many little animals are scared out of their wits at nights when the family sits around fireplaces reading the story of The Three Little Pigs? Right here in Maplewood, when Mr. Wolf dares to venture out in public, children run, scream, and hide from him. This is no quality of life for an upright law-abiding citizen such as Mr. Wolf.

"It is high time that the culprits who operate this moneymaking machine pay restitution to the wolf community which has long suffered in silence. Members of the jury, these lying pigs are still collecting royalties off their lying story. The honorable thing to do is to right the terrible wrong they have done and end the nightmare to which they have subjected my client. I also want to thank you members of the jury for your time and patience over these past weeks. Now I ask that you use your wisdom and sense of fairness to find the pigs liable for defaming Mr. Wolf. If you do, you will be fulfilling your civic duty and allowing an innocent wolf to get back what was taken from him so many years ago: his good name and the good name of his family, his children, and his children's children." With that, Counsel Boar walked to his seat, took out his handkerchief, and wiped his sweaty face.

The audience could not ignore Counsel Boar's riveting summation of the case. The Three Pigs felt uneasy and they bowed their heads in contemplation. Now they were not so sure of a victory after all. Some of the pigs scowled disapprovingly at Counsel Boar; they would never forgive him for being an outright sellout.

Straw House Pig had one response to make in her closing argument. "The wolf is a liar, members of the jury, so you must not believe the lying Mr. Wolf and his lawyer.

"The '*big bad wolf*' IS A LIAR,'" she screamed as high as her decibels could go.

CHAPTER THIRTY-SIX

JURY INSTRUCTION

The Judge gave the jury members their instructions before they filed out of the courtroom. In his instructions, he warned them they were not to speak to the press or to anyone else about their deliberations.

"All bias has to be left outside, and the jury's decision should be based strictly on the facts and nothing else," said Judge Hognott.

"Members of the jury, you must remember that the burden to prove defamation lies on the plaintiff, Mr. Wolf. Remember, this is a case about defamation. Defamation, according to the law, is the wrongful hurting of a person's reputation. In other words, communication is defamatory if it tends to lower a person's standing in the community or if it deters a third person from associating or dealing with the person who is defamed."

The Judge said that the law imposed a requirement that people refrain from making false, defamatory statements about others. He also stated that when a person orally breached this duty, this was the tort of slander. If the breach is in writing, that is the tort of libel. "Defamation occurs," Judge Hognott said, "When a false statement is made about a person, his or her business, or property. Second, the plaintiff must prove that the Defendants, The Three Pigs, published the statements, meaning The Three Pigs made false statement to other persons about the Plaintiff, Mr. Wolf." The Judge looked straight at The Three Pigs as he stated this. "Furthermore, the Plaintiff must also prove by a preponderance of the evidence that it is more likely than not that the defendants, The Three Pigs, lied on Mr. Wolf." The Judge then instructed the jury members to ask themselves the following questions:

1.   Did the Defendants, The Three Pigs, make a false statement about Mr. Wolf?
2.   If yes, then you must answer the next question. Did The Three Pigs communicate or tell this lie to a third party other than to Mr. Wolf? If you find yes, the third question you must answer is
3.   Did this lie cause harm to the reputation of the Plaintiff, Mr. Wolf? Jurors, remember that unless you have evidence to the contrary, we must assume that Mr. Wolf had a good name and reputation prior to the defamation at issue. If you believe this to be true, you must find The Three Pigs liable of defamation.

The snickers of pigs echoed through the courtroom as the Judge uttered these statements about Mr. Wolf's reputation.

One pig was brave enough to yell, "FIND THE PIGS NOT LIABLE THEN."

Court officers tossed that pig out of the courtroom as the wolves cheered his removal. Judge Hognott, clearly not amused and coming to the end of his rope, yelled,

"I AM THIS CLOSE TO EMPTYING THIS COURTROOM OF SPECTATORS."

The courtroom became deadly silent. If a pin had dropped, you would have heard it.

However, the Judge continued his discourse while looking at the jurors.

"A defense to defamation is truth; consequently, if you believe that the defendants The Three Pigs were telling the truth as it relates to the Plaintiff, Mr. Wolf, then you must find The Three Pigs not liable—meaning not responsible for any harm Mr. Wolf may have suffered."

One pig whispered, "Amen" so low that only the wolf sitting next to her heard and promptly elbowed her. The pig shut her mouth and decided to keep the rest of her thoughts to herself. The Judge was not going to toss her out of the courtroom on the last day of the trial, when all her nosy neighbors, Peggy Sue, Penny, and Minny Mouse, were waiting for her to recount the court happenings. The pig had become somewhat of a minor celebrity in her neighborhood because of her access to the trial of the wolf and The Three Pigs. Before dawn, every day she was up. She was the first one in line to get into court. She had been lucky enough to persuade her mother to watch the little ones in her absence. Usually no one paid her much attention. Many of her friends considered her a boring homemaker who only stayed home and mothered her three piglets. Often she had nothing to say to her husband when he came home from a hard day's work at Billyboys except to complain about what antics the three little piglets were involved in around the house. Her husband usually paid her little attention as he flipped the remote from channel to channel.

However, lately her husband had rushed home to listen to her tales from the courtroom. Therefore, she was not going to mess up her chance of seeing the rest of the trial because of the stupid wolf sitting next to her. Further, if she elbowed him back, he would probably club her to death. Mr. Wolf and the wolf sitting next to her had proven beyond the shadow of a doubt that wolves were most dangerous. Clearly, this was why The Three Pigs were in this predicament. The pig took a deep breath to calm down and tried to listen to what the Judge was saying while ignoring her own *"big bad wolf"* sitting dangerously close right next to her.

Judge Hognott also warned the jurors that they would be sequestered—meaning no communication with anyone outside of the jury pool. The jurors could not go home during the deliberation process. Instead, the Judge ordered that they stay at a hotel. He again reiterated that the jurors were not to discuss the trial with anyone outside of the Judge and other jurors. This included Facebook, Twitter, or any social networking site. The Judge warned the jurors about the confidentiality of the proceedings. The warning did not apply to the spectators, so many of the pigs and wolves who watched the trial went out and tweeted the day's events.

The Judge then gave the oath to the Bailiff. "Do you solemnly affirm that you will escort these jurors to the designated room and keep them there, and you will allow absolutely no one to speak to them, and that you will not speak to them without the court's permission, except to ask them whether they have agreed on a verdict?"

The Bailiff turned solemnly to the Judge and said,

"Your Honor, I agree." The Bailiff beamed proudly as all eyes were on him as he took this solemn pledge.

Finally, Judge Hognott looked at the spectators in the courtroom and said, "This suspends these proceedings till the verdict comes in. That is all, folks," he quipped with as much humor as he had ever displayed before walking rapidly out of the courtroom. He did not stop to have a conversation with anyone, not even the reporters who tried to talk to him about the trial. Many of the spectators rushed out of the courtroom, eager to talk about the last day of the trial with any reporter willing to listen.

Lawyers, legal experts, and talking heads from all over the land bombarded every news media on the evening news to predict the outcome of the case. Some said it did not look good for The Three Pigs, while others said the wolf did not present enough evidence to convince the jurors, the Judge, or the public of his innocence. Catchy headlines in the morning papers attracted a large audience. *The Daily Reporter*, a mediocre newspaper, for example, sold out every copy that went to press that day.

CHAPTER THIRTY-SEVEN

DELIBERATION

The jury comprised of seven pigs, three foxes, and two wolves, as per the judge's order remained sequestered at the Fox Inn Hotel. The media camped out around the clock near their location. There was even talk in the press that some of the jurors were already writing their memoirs about the case. Each day court personnel transported the jurors via the court van to continue their deliberations in the jury room located at the back of the courthouse. It was a simple medium-sized room, painted white and devoid of any decorations. Right over the doorway hung a large clock that rather loudly ticked the minutes away. The jurors had to walk in single file to the large rectangular table with matching chairs in the center of the room. The chairs were comfortable, and the foxes and wolves seemed to huddle closely together on one side, while the pigs sat on the other side. On the first day of the trial, they elected Mrs. Snout as the jury forepig. She was middle-aged with a good sense of humor. Mrs. Snout was clearly the most respected of the bunch.

Mrs. Snout addressed the jurors in a respectful and no-nonsense manner as she sat back in her wheelchair.

"Members of the jury, I feel honored that you saw fit to appoint me to such an honorable position. I crave your cooperation in the smooth running of this process. We are here to execute a very important duty, and it is incumbent on us to do so fairly and respectfully without prejudice or malice. We do have our own beliefs and biases, but remember the Judge's instructions. The Judge has passed the baton to us to complete the last leg of this journey. I admonish you to respect one another's right to speak, to respect all opinions and viewpoints, to review and follow the jury instructions, and to examine all evidence with an open mind. Remember the longevity of this process is dependent on all of us, and the earlier we reach a just conclusion, the better, so please let us expedite the process."

Despite the appeal made by the jury forepig, chaos ensued from day one. The bad blood from the trial had spilled over into the jury pool, and it was hard to imagine how both sides of this animal divide could reconcile their differences amicably. Mrs. Snout surveyed the audience and immediately felt disheartened. She wondered what she could do to diffuse the toxic atmosphere that tainted the jury. The wolves were upset because they felt the selection process had been unfair. The fact of the matter is that the pigs outnumbered the wolves more than three to one. Ms. Snout again reiterated that they had to make a quick decision because she wanted to get back to her family. "I know this is also your intention," she said, "because we have been away from our families long enough." She was trying to rally everyone's support by appealing to everyone's love of family.

A pig called Curly Sue, who talked between chewing and popping gum, said that rendering a fair verdict should not be a problem because everyone knew the wolf was guilty. She said,

"I mean, who didn't read the story of <u>The Three Little Pigs</u> and <u>Little Red Riding Hood</u>? I read those stories countless times, and it is quite clear that the wolf..."

One of the wolves, Mr. Furly, who took his job as a jury member seriously, interrupted her and stated that because she thought the wolf was guilty because of the books she read, her bias had no place in the jury room.

"This case," Mr. Furly said, "should be based on facts, and only facts. That is what the Judge advised."

Mr. Furly looked at Curly Sue quite sternly and at the other jurors, hoping for their approval, but they stared at him in obstinate silence. Curly Sue backed down somewhat as she looked at Mr. Furly, who seemed ready to explode with disgust. The other pigs exchanged side-glances, knowing they would confer amongst themselves later. One of the pigs thought it was a lucky break for pigs because they outnumbered the wolves.

The tension in the jury room seemed to have gotten decidedly hotter, and Mrs. Snout thought it was a pity she could not blog about this apparent unfolding drama in real time. However, she could not risk it. The Judge would throw her off the jury for such improprieties. Mrs. Snout remembered that she was in charge of the proceedings, and she had to maintain order.

"Jury members," she said in her most commanding voice, "We are here to do a job. Let's get it done."

The rest of the first night of jury deliberation went somewhat smoothly after that, as the wolves and the pigs watched each other warily. Mr. Furly was the only juror who appeared to have been listening to the Judge's instructions. The rest of the jurors seemed to have already made up their minds according to their respective biases, and they stubbornly refused to budge an inch, not even in the name of fairness or justice.

On the second day of jury deliberation, contention still reigned. It was clear the process would not be easy. The pigs all clustered in one corner, while the majority of the canine family stood on the other side of the room. Noting this, the jury forepig sighed, knowing that the jury deliberation process would most likely entail many bumps in the road. It would most likely derail Mrs. Snout's plans of getting this verdict over with so she could get back to her family. She looked at the twelve jurors with as much confidence as she could muster, watching the proceedings carefully as she tried to assess and gauge each juror's possible vote. She took note of Mr. Furly and remembered his argument from the previous day. She hoped he would not be a problem, since he seemed bent on following the law. She observed the very obese Curly Sue, who was busy stuffing her mouth with candy, seemingly oblivious to the tension enveloping the room. From the conversations they had had over dinner, she knew that Curly Sue was quite ditsy. Mrs. Snout knew she could persuade Curly Sue to her way of thinking.

One of the foxes looked at Mrs. Snout quite contemptuously and said,

"What are we waiting for? Let us vote and get on with our lives. I have a business to run. I already wasted several weeks of my life listening to endless testimonies."

"I second that," said another wolf in the room.

Mrs. Snout decided she had to take charge immediately, so she told the jurors they would do a secret ballot to determine where each juror stood on the liability of The Three Pigs. The pigs laughed heartily at what they considered a preposterous idea. Mrs. Snout looked at the jurors with a confidence she did not feel and proceeded to hand out the ballots to the other jurors. The pigs on the jury giggled gleefully when they filled out their ballot as if they had their own little secret. Mr. Furly seemed to be in quiet contemplation as he filled out his ballot.

Curly Sue, who was sitting by herself, was busy twisting her tight curls while popping her gum. She wondered how she should vote, so she tried to think logically. It was an established fact that wolves were known to be dangerous; therefore, Mr. Wolf had to be dangerous. She even remembered someone speaking about Red Riding Hood and the wolf at the trial. Curly Sue thought about the little pig from the straw house, but she had not looked too convincing on the witness stand. Curly Sue made up her mind and voted. After everyone voted, Mrs. Snout counted the votes. She almost cried when she saw the results. It appeared the jurors were in for the long haul, and the night would just be the beginning of many more long nights to come.

As the deliberation process wore on, The Three Little Pigs' supporters accused the Judge of showing bad judgment by letting the jurors stay at the Fox Inn Hotel. The wolf supporters called the whole court a kangaroo court bent on hiding the truth, considering there were seven pigs and two wolves on the jury. Some even argued that foxes were part of the dog family and that gave Mr. Wolf an unfair advantage.

The Judge gave the jurors five days to come up with a verdict, but after five days, the forepig wrote the Judge asking for an extension of time because they were still deliberating the case. The Judge granted them more time as requested.

During the jury deliberation process, the media obtained pictures of some of the jurors swimming in the hotel pool and ordering expensive meals while wrapped in white hotel bath towels. The cameras caught two of the pigs on the jury getting pedicures while three other pigs waited in the hotel spa to get expensive mud massages with what appeared to be volcanic stones. Hotel management gave the penthouse suite to the foxes on the jury, according to reputable sources. The two wolves were also spending a considerable amount of time at the hotel pool, according to the evening news. The media also reported seeing jurors at a club partying right on the hotel's premises.

A video reportedly acquired for about $50,000 and shown by TMZ captured the following grainy outtake. "This is DJ Wolf Paws on the ones and twos. Now I am going to drop the hottest joint on the dance floor...It's called..." Before the DJ could complete his spiel, the wolves and foxes in the club, including those from the jury, started to nod their heads in unison to the pulsating beat before hitting the dance floor. The wolves and foxes in a synchronized fashion with their mouths pointed in the air danced to the beat and words of

"Do the huffy puffy, do the huffy puffy....Put your heads in the air and howl cause you just don't care. Do the huffy puffy, do the huffy puffy. Put your mouths in the air as if you just don't care. Do the huffy puffy, do the huffy puffy."

For twenty minutes, the pigs watched this charade in fascination until DJ Paws turned his headphones over to DJ Snout, a pig wearing a red and white sports suit with white sneakers. DJ Snazzy shouted into the microphone resting on top of the turntable.

"OK, Paws, you did ya thing, now let's start the party right," he said in a somewhat sarcastic voice.

He stood upright on his hind legs, waved one hoof in the air while dancing to the beat, and yelled,

"Where my pigs at?" The pigs responded with grunts and snorts of approval as he started playing an extremely popular hit often played on piggy rotations on many radio stations and MTV.

"Piggy jig jog…Piggy jig jog, I hop like a frog, but I'm proud to be a hog. Piggy jig jog…Piggy jig jog. I hop like a frog, but I'm proud to be a hog. Piggy jig jog…Piggy jig jog."

All the pigs, including those from the jury, fell in line on the dance floor and gyrated in a slow running jog. They hopped like frogs and continued their fancy dance steps, two steps forward, then hopping like a frog. The star of the show, however, was Curly Sue, who seemed to let loose all her pent-up energy. As she danced, she rocked back and forth violently, stuck out her fat rounded rump, and wiggled her tail vigorously. Curly Sue swayed her large hips from side to side in sync with the music while squealing the lyrics at the top of her lungs. The wolves appeared stunned by the display of such charged energy, and from the sidelines, they too rocked to the rhythmic thumping of the hypnotic beat.

However, because the club was dark and the video was so grainy, it was not clear who was in the club. This would have been a violation of the sequestration order, but all the jurors denied stepping foot in the Fox nightclub or knowing any of the songs featured in the video. As a result, Judge Hognott warned angrily that if he heard about any further shenanigans, he would start dismissing jurors. All the jurors nodded their heads in agreement, promising to focus on the task at hand, which was deliberating the fate of The Three Pigs. As they listened, the wolves, foxes, and pigs glanced accusingly at each other, but sighed since they had avoided the worst—which was being disgraced and dismissed as jurors. To make sure no other impropriety occurred, the Judge ordered guards to watch the jurors' for the balance of their deliberation. Weary groans were heard from the jurors at this pronouncement.

As the deliberation process continued, Maplewood was abuzz with the usual day-to-day activities. The barbershops especially attracted many customers. Between shaved beards, trimmed furs, and haircuts, there were contentious arguments about the outcome of the case. In beauty salons, female pigs and wolves had their hair shampooed, blow-dried, and colored as they gossiped and debated the outcome of the trial. The steam from the hair dryers seemed to equal the heated discussions filtering through the salons. In several instances, salon owners physically booted customers from the salons as arguments turned physical.

Manicurists fared no better. They had to suffer through loud arguments and counter arguments among customers about the case as they snipped, glued, and manicured hoof and paw nails. Post-trial commentators on radio and television seemed to outtalk each other and add to the frenzy of the moment as the workers patiently went through the motions.

In butcher shops across town, wolves who were butchers clad in their white jackets ground meat from unknown sources as they nervously glanced at the news occasionally. At colleges, the case became a learning experience as law professors engaged their students in discussions about the trial. The constant face-offs between wolves and pigs drove a deep wedge between them that further exacerbated an already volatile situation in the town of Maplewood.

During the deliberation process, Mr. Wolf stayed close to home, only wandering occasionally to the local café. His main source of company was Mrs. Wolf and his children, who visited from time to time but sometimes seemed deterred by the chaos brewing outside their home caused by the press. Mrs. Wolf upset at her self- inflicted imprisonment at home busied herself with her favorite soap operas *The Young and the Foxy*, and *Maplewood Doctors*. Every time Mrs. Wolf ventured outside, the paparazzi ambushed her while the news media camped out around her house as they waited for the verdict.

One thing Mr. Wolf could be grateful for was that the house was spotless. Mrs. Wolf was bored out of her mind after watching countless hours of media outtakes, so she scrubbed and licked the place immaculately clean. Out of frustration, she knitted several sweaters for her grandchildren and half finished a sweater for Mr. Wolf.

Mrs. Wolf had even gotten Mr. Wolf to apply a fresh coat of paint to the bedroom. Glad to get rid of his nervous energy, Mr. Wolf had acquiesced. However, he made a mess of everything, and Mrs. Wolf felt she should have left well alone. Rather than a good paint job, he left large splotches on the wall that worsened the condition of the room. Mrs. Wolf knew that next time; she would just hire a professional painter. She even wishfully thought that if the verdict turned out right, they could buy a new house. She smiled at this thought as she continued to knit, despite the cabin fever she had to endure.

More days passed and still the jury had not reached a verdict. The media was scrambling for news of what was going on, but mum was the word.

CHAPTER THIRTY-EIGHT

THE VERDICT

A fter two weeks of deliberation, the jurors sent a message to the Judge that they had arrived at a decision. The news channels all issued an alert that flashed "Breaking News" across the TV screens: "The jury has finally reached a verdict in the case of *Mr. Wolf v. The Three Pigs.*" Media personnel and interested citizens immediately rushed to the courthouse to hear the verdict firsthand. Usually the courthouse area was filled to capacity. However, on this day, there was an overflow in the halls and outside of the courthouse as throngs of spectators waited for the outcome. The judge ordered all court officers to work since chaos seemed likely if crowd control was not put into effect.

Judge Hognott eventually entered the courtroom hastily. He had been playing a game of golf with some of the other judges and some law-yers when he received a call concerning the verdict. In his haste, his black robe sheltered his golfing outfit. Judge Hognott hurried off the course, raced to his grey Bentley, and threw his golfing paraphernalia on the backseat. His driver sped to the courthouse, not wanting to invoke the displeasure of the Judge, who could be most disagreeable at times. Judge Hognott's toupee now twisted sideways, so he had to find some hairpins to pin it down the best way he could until he could meet with his stylist, Haveere. The white golfing sneakers that peeked out under the Judge's black robe were a stark contrast to his usual conservative attire. Peeved at being disturbed during his game, Judge Hognott appeared meaner than his usually surly self. He wanted to make this quick and sweet, and he was not too happy that he had to wait for the jurors to arrive. Ten minutes later, the jurors filed in, their expressions unreadable. Because of Judge Hognott's many years of experience on the bench, he sensed he was not about to like the outcome one bit. After the jurors sat in their seats, the court officer announced, "The matter of *Mr. Wolf v. The Three Pigs* in the Superior Court of Maplewood is now in session."

The Judge looked at the jurors and asked in a booming voice. "Have you reached a verdict?" The attorneys with their respective clients remained seated in the front row as they stared expectedly at the jurors. Mr. Wolf, seated right next to Counsel Boar, felt as if his heart had crawled up in his throat. The clock in the courtroom seemed to tick rather loudly as everyone waited anxiously for the verdict. Finally, the jury forepig, Mrs. Snout, stood up and handed a piece of paper to the Bailiff, who in turn handed the paper to the Judge.

The Judge's face registered dismay as he looked at the white sheet of paper. He blinked twice as if to clear his vision. He rubbed his eyes, wiped the sweat from his face, and shouted in a booming voice that echoed loudly through the courtroom, "SO, MEMBERS OF THE JURY, AFTER TWO WEEKS OF DELIBERATION, YOU HAVE STILL NOT BEEN ABLE TO COME TO DECISION? "

Some of the jurors jumped in fright as they faced the wrath of the Judge.

"No, Your Honor," said the jury fore pig shakily as she shivered in her wheelchair.

Mrs. Snout weakly replied, "Your Honor, everyone was just taking sides and did not seem to care about the truth of the matter. After a while, we were just going in circles without covering any new ground. The foxes and wolves thought the pigs were lying, and the pigs believed the wolf was lying. It has been that way since we started deliberating. Your Honor, it doesn't appear this will change two weeks later, a month later, or even a year later." Mrs. Snout spoke calmly even in the face of Judge Hognott's wrath. "So, Your Honor, we are helplessly and hopelessly deadlocked."

The Judge was visibly upset, but knew there was nothing he could do but to announce a mistrial. Pandemonium instantly broke out in the court as each side started yelling at the other. The Judge slammed down his gavel, and yelled, "ORDER IN THE COURT."

He then calmly told the jurors,

"We the citizens of Maplewood thank you for your time over the very arduous weeks of this trial. Thank you again for your service. You have the right to speak to the media or not to—that is your choice. You have the right to speak freely. You also have your right to privacy. Remember, reporters in the media will try to find out how you came to this decision, and you may speak to them or you may chose not to speak. If you choose to, you may endanger your life since some will question your judgment. Jurors, you are now dismissed," Judge Hognott said, already bored with the whole proceeding.

He just wanted to see the last of this case and head for his well-deserved vacation. As Judge Hognott exited the courtroom, some of the wolves stared stonily at the pigs on the jury while the pigs fiercely glared back.

CHAPTER THIRTY-NINE

MAPLEWOOD REACTS

Once the verdict transmitted around the country and the world, media frenzy escalated to an all-time high. Reporters hurried back and forth hoping to catch a glimpse of the jurors and parties involved in the case. Outside the courthouse, police wearing riot gear had assembled to keep in check the angry protesters brandishing provocative placards. The police placed barricades around the courthouse steps while armed officers checked for any sign of trouble as different reactions to the verdict were swiftly forthcoming.

At the prestigious Hog University (also known as HU) located in the heart of Maplewood, students sat impatiently as the thick warm air enveloped the room. In one particular lecture room, time seemed to stand still as the professor droned on about history. Many of the students felt the verdict in the case of *Mr. Wolf v. The Three Pigs* was much more relevant than the present lecture. The college pigs that were in the middle of a history lecture were impatiently checking their cell phones as they anxiously awaited the verdict. Professor Surley, replete with maps and a smart board, droned on about the civil war between the pigs and the wolves that had occurred centuries ago. As soon as the verdict flashed across their cell phone screens, many students clad in their customary T-shirts and jeans jumped up and high-fived one another, yelling,

"HA! HA! THE WICKED WOLF DID NOT PREVAIL."

The old hunchbacked professor, upset that his lecture had been disturbed, told them sternly,

"Put those phones away!"

The students hurriedly scooping up their laptops, books, and backpacks drowned out his command. Students who ignored his stern command hurried away to watch the courthouse happenings via the big-screen TV in the student lounge. The students who remained seated continued texting, so the professor resignedly gave up teaching and promptly dismissed the class. "I hate technology; those gadgets are nothing but weapons of distraction," the professor griped. "I long for the good old days when students were eager to learn, common sense prevailed, and students were not so addicted to texting." How can a professor compete with the gadgets that hold the young spellbound? He wondered as he glanced around the empty classroom. Professor Surley sighed as he grabbed his lecture notes and sauntered out of the room. Maybe next semester would be better, or maybe he was just getting too old for this, he thought as he walked slowly to his car.

At school, playgrounds across the county, little piggies did the piggy jig jog while some of the wolves watched in distaste. Many of them clearly upset at the verdict. Some of the wolves and foxes, however, were happy with the verdict, knowing they would maintain their reputation as dangerous creatures that you had better not mess with.

On numerous highways, traffic slowed to a halt when drivers heard the verdict. Some yelled their agreement through their car windows while others honked their horns loudly. In malls across Maplewood and beyond, shoppers momentarily paused as they heard the verdict, but quickly resumed shopping for the latest designer brands or discounts. In Maplewood Square, the verdict flashed boldly across the giant TV screens positioned at strategic locations. Some viewers jumped for joy, while other stared in disbelief. Even Maplewood's stock market took a dive as stockbrokers dressed in Ralph Lauren black label, Armani suits, and Brooks Brothers had waged bets on the outcome of the trial. The losers paid up their dues and others shook their heads in disbelief for not foreseeing this outcome. After the winners boasted and others cheered, the floor resumed its chaotic exchange as they bought and sold stocks for their clients.

Far away on a distant highway, one lone wolf rider atop his black shiny Harley-Davidson motorcycle smiled and shouted a loud hurrah as the verdict reached him on the long stretch of road. He revved up his engine, increased his speed, and tried to outrun the sun. His signature black jacket flashed in the dusk as if in celebration of his perceived victory. As he disappeared into the dustup, the word *Stalker* emblazoned on his jacket revealed his identity and seemed to merge the painful past with the present. While Mr. Wolf endeavored to flee the past, Stalker was just as eager to embrace it. The past for Stalker meant power, respect, and self-actualization, and he saw no need for change.

Outside of the courtroom, Ms. Priggly proudly posed in a bright fuchsia Versace suit, a matching fuchsia wide-brimmed hat, and dark Dolce and Gabbana sunglasses. The Three Pigs surrounded Ms. Priggly.

"I am quite happy with the verdict," she told reporters.

She smiled broadly, looked into the cameras and said, "The truth was clearly on our side.

The Jurors were clearly too smart to fall for Mr. Wolf's silly lies. The nerve of him to think that my clients would have to dole out even a penny to pay him for attempted murder."

"Not so!" yelled a wolf quite loudly, who was standing closely behind her.

"The jury was just stacked with too many pigs, so what did you expect?" he asked. Another wolf yelled, "A wolf can never get a fair trial in a town overrun with prejudiced pigs."

Ms. Priggly faltered briefly at this outburst before she resumed talking to the reporters. "THANK YOU, EVERYONE," she yelled to the crowd gathered outside the courtroom.

"What's next, Ms. Priggly?" some of the reporters asked.

Ms. Priggly replied, "Just wait and see," as she winked at them playfully.

"The Three Pigs and I thank you," she said as she hurried away.

She was exhilarated and flushed with her perceived victory in the courtroom. The Three Pigs smiled happily, as they surrounded Mrs. Priggly and then jumped into an awaiting pink car that instantly whisked them away to celebrate their victory. For the moment, it appeared all animosity between the three seemingly forgotten.

Counsel Boar appeared visibly upset as he stood outside the courthouse. He thanked supporters for their patience, but went on to disagree with the outcome of the case. He smiled broadly, as he told the audience of mainly dogs and wolves that the jury verdict showed that enough jurors believed the wolf to hang the jury. However, Counsel Boar explained that the jury had been heavily stacked against the wolf and for the next trial; he would request a change of venue, perhaps in federal court.

"This is clearly pig country, and I should know," Counsel Boar chuckled.

The audience did not seem quite as amused at his jokes, so Counsel Boar stopped chuckling and became serious. He said,

"Remember folks, this is not the end," as if trying to convince himself and the others standing around that there was still hopes of vindication for the wolf community.

Mr. Wolf and Mrs. Wolf, on the other hand, were quite subdued as they walked from the courthouse, both shocked at the outcome. Mrs. Wolf turned to Mr. Wolf and said quietly,

"Mr. Wolf, we will get those pigs the next time."

Mr. Wolf just looked at her and nodded his head in disbelief about the verdict. As they walked home paw in paw, their head noisy with confused thoughts, they knew that once again justice had eluded them.

Mrs. Wolf was brimming with disappointment as she imagined the new house they could have bought, all the clothes she could have ordered from catalogues, and the goodies she could have purchased if the verdict had been in Mr. Wolf's favor. She had become enthusiastic about the lawsuit when she realized Mr. Wolf could have won millions. She wondered if things would ever go back to the way it had been before the trial. Only time would tell.

Counsel Boar was thinking about the time he spent preparing for this case and how much work he would have to do for a retrial. Thus far, Counsel Boar had not made money on this case as he thought he would; however, nothing could compensate for all the publicity he was getting. For example, tonight he had an appearance on Fox News. Already, he was thinking about the suit he would wear. Helping Mr. Wolf was turning out to be a good thing for his career.

Mr. Wolf was most despondent about the verdict; however, he was determined not to give up. He wondered if he would ever clear his name. Maybe in the next trial, the jury would be stacked with more wolves, and the hand of justice would finally favor him.

The morning following the trial, the printed news posted a colorful array of interesting headlines. An unflattering picture of Mr.Wolf with sheep's clothing lying at his feet posted under a headline that read, "**Out of the Closet at Last**" in the *Reader's Choice*. The *Truth of the Matter* headlines read, "**Gotcha Again**" under an illustration showing three smiling pigs with guns trained on a helpless, bleeding wolf leaning against a tree. Paper pigs and wolves loudly peddled their newspapers in the street, shouting, and "Extra! Extra! Read all about it." Needless to say, they made a tidy sum of money because in record time the newsstands were empty.

The next night, one juror who only identified herself as Juror Number Five due to the numerous death threats against the jurors, made an appearance on *Headline News*. She looked quite different from anyone who had served as a juror on the case of *Mr. Wolf v. The Three Pigs*.

Juror Number 5 was all Guccied out in a lilac strapless dress with gold stiletto heels. The Juror's newly weaved hair cascaded past her waist almost to the ground, and her face buried deep in makeup. Fake eye-lashes dripped a deep black dye that trickled dangerously close to her nose. Her lips glistened with a ghastly shiny purple lip-gloss that tainted objects that came too close. Large sparkling earrings dangled from her ears like chandeliers, and her white Gucci sunglasses glittered with the many rhinestones embedded in the frames.

Those who were watching the news thought Juror Number 5 looked like she had just flown in from Hollywood. Sitting next to her was her newly hired publicist who spent her days auctioning off Juror Number Five's media appearance to the highest bidders. Juror Number 5, in hushed tones, said she would only talk about what transpired in the jury deliberation in her book, _Confessions of a Juror_, due out in the coming weeks. The publicist quickly ended the interview and rushed Juror Number Five out of the studio as she headed to her next appearance. Some of the jurors watching _Headline News_ thought Juror Number Five looked very familiar, but they could not be sure of her identity. Some said she had a startling resemblance to Curly Sue. Not to be outdone, a few of the other jurors hired publicists, so they could secure a spot on one of the news stations. Other jurors remained in hiding, due to the death threats they saw online in response to the verdict.

CHAPTER FORTY

IS THIS THE END?

As days moved into weeks and then months, the Town of Maplewood returned to some sense of normalcy. The pigs kept to themselves on their side of the street, while the wolves and foxes silently watched, ready to pounce at the slightest provocation. The older pigs kept a watchful eye on the canines. They could not trust that the newly established peace would remain intact. However, from time to time, some of the citizens of Maplewood enjoyed recounting the story of *Mr. Wolf v. The Three Pigs.* Some believed the saga could not possibility be over and waited impatiently for the next chapter to unfold.

The clock in the town square ticked on while pedestrians clothed in their fall jackets hurried about their business along the concrete sidewalks. Life in Maplewood was like any other neighborhood. Everyone was concerned about money. Nannies pushed their charges to their next appointments. Parents worried about what meals they would prepare for dinner, as the citizens of Maplewood waited anxiously for the next big story to hit the airways.

MR. WOLF V. THE THREE PIGS

Far away from the center of Maplewood, as day turned into night in the heart of the forest, Mr. Wolf lay in his bed, wrapped in his graham-checkered sheet as he snacked on a granola bar. He was wearing his favorite grey and red striped pajamas, which his wife had given him for a Christmas present. He reflected on the events of the past year and a half. The excitement of the trial had died down, and the noisy reporters who had camped out on his lawn were long gone. He was an old wolf now, but he thought of earlier times when he was young and life held promise. He resigned himself to a fate he seemed incapable of changing. The lifelong perplexing questions to which he had no answer kept tugging at his heart: "Will I get my name back? Will the children of my loins continue to bear the scorn of society, or will they be relieved of the yoke of discrimination and injustice?" Only time would tell. Mr. Wolf sighed wearily, glanced at the clock, and then looked at a snoring Mrs. Wolf, his soul mate and life's companion, sleeping next to him. He gave her a loving peck on the cheek, and she rolled over and muttered sleepy gibberish. These intense thoughts seemed to exhaust him, and he drifted off to sleep, as the clock seemed to tick a rhythmic lullaby. Tomorrow would be another day, and perchance the wheels of justice would turn in his favor and free him and his posterity from the prison of natural circumstances that had held them captive all their lives. In dreamland, Mr. Wolf seemed to reach for an elusive deferred dream as he geared up for the challenges ahead.

To Be Continued- Maybe